Lost Time

Lost Time

Between Two Evils Trilogy
Book Two

DL Orton

ROCKY MOUNTAIN PRESS

Accolades Paper

A Publishers Weekly Great Indie Star
Readers' Favorite Book Award Winner
Indie Excellence Book Award Winner
Indie Book Awards Finalist
International Book Awards Finalist

"Engaging, Funny, Romantic & Harrowing!"
Publishers Weekly Starred Review

"Exceptionally Well Written & Deftly Crafted"
Midwest Book Review

"Rich, Detailed, Fast-Paced & Intelligent"
Literary Picks

"The Best Sci-Fi Love Story of the Year!"
Panda Books

"Edgy, Literary, Pithy & Refreshingly Naughty!"
E.M. Davis, Senior Editor @ Pressque

"I was satisfied, exhausted, inspired, and blown away."
J. Staughton, Sheriff Nottingham eLit Magazine

To My Readers-

Dots of ink lie dormant in an unread book,
Waiting,
Like black holes into another universe,
For someone to find them
And engage the warp drive.

Thank you!
I love you guys.

When you are courting a nice girl,
An hour seems like a second.
When you sit on a red-hot cinder,
A second seems like an hour.
That's relativity.

~Albert Einstein

Chapter 1

Diego: Out on a Limb

I lie in greenish half-light, my lungs on fire, panic forcing out any rational thought. And then I remember where I am. Or rather where I am supposed to be. I pound my fists against the translucent coffin until I manage to hit the release lever. The lid pops opens and frigid air rushes in, smelling of damp, rotting leaves. I gasp for breath.

I lie still for a few moments, inhaling the clammy air and waiting for my pulse to stop pounding in my ears. The last thing I remember before everything went black is a panicked voice shouting to abort the mission. Stop the countdown because...

Shit. I can't remember. But it definitely wasn't good.

I lift my head and a blinding pain stabs me in the forehead. I take a forced breath, pushing down the urge to vomit, and open my eyes. All my body parts seem to be attached, but my skin is unnaturally wrinkled, like I stayed in the ocean for hours.

I collapse back into the cold capsule and notice the blood spattered across the lid. Now that I think about it, I can feel the cut in my right palm, probably from the sharp spines of the damn seashell.

I wipe my hand on the cheap towel and shudder. The air is too cold and damp for the beach.

Where the hell am I?

I take a deep breath. It doesn't smell like La Isla beach, either. Maybe I missed the target and landed in the rainforest?

At least I didn't arrive underwater.

I lie still, listening for the sound of the surf, but hear nothing except a low-pitched groan. The capsule is tipping ever so slightly. I gather my strength and kick the lid off. It bangs and crashes as it falls away from the pod, taking a long time to land.

I force my near-sighted eyes to focus. Above me, massive coniferous branches fan out, fog rolling in just beyond the treetops.

This is definitely not the tropics.

I heave myself up high enough to see over the side of the capsule, shivering in the damp, chilly air. The pod is lodged in the upper boughs of a giant tree, perhaps thirty meters above the blurry fern-covered forest floor.

Shit, I hate heights.

The soft groan becomes louder and the pod shifts beneath me.

Mierda. Let's do this before it's too late.

I rush to get out before the branch gives way, but my muscles aren't working properly, and it's harder than I expect. I manage to wrench myself out on the third try, but as I climb over the edge of the pod, my towel slips off and lodges a couple of limbs below me. I put my bare feet down on to the moss-covered bark, grab onto a higher branch, and pull myself up, glancing down at my shriveled privates.

Whose idea was it to send me in a towel? Shorts would have been a lot more practical.

There's a cold breeze, and the fog is getting thicker by the minute. If I don't get down before it gets dark...

Let's not go there.

I shuffle sideways along the slippery branch until I reach the relative safety of the trunk, and then take a moment to look around. The world is green as far as I can see. The only exception is what must be a blue body of water floating where the hills meet the horizon. There is not a person, house, car, road, or other sign of human life anywhere.

Something moves at the edge of my vision, and when I look more carefully, the trees seem to be crawling with giant bugs! I blink a couple of times and realize that they're not insects, but large, black birds—hundreds of them perched in every tree. I shut my eyes for a moment, pushing down vertigo, and then start climbing down, naked and shivering, trying to figure out how the hell I ended up in Alfred Hitchcock's nightmare.

I believe the trees are redwoods, but I'm not particularly good with plant identification. It occurs to me that Isabel would know, and a wave of despair sweeps over me. I try to shake it off and concentrate on the problem at hand. In any case, they are definitely not the sort of trees that grow in the tropics—at least not in my time. Now that I think about it, it does look a lot like the Jurassic forests you see in dinosaur movies.

Mierda.

I look out across the forest again, dread creeping up my exposed back. My whole body is shaking, and I feel weak. No tyrannosaurs or brachiosaurs; nothing but green—and all those birds! Birds descended from dinosaurs, so I probably don't need to worry about being eaten by a velociraptor, but I can't remember if there were ever giant, man-eating dodos.

The redwood is huge, and I have to shinny sideways around the trunk to find foot and hand holds, causing my naked frontside to bump and scrape against the rough bark.

Note to self: The Hitchhiker's Guide was wrong. When time traveling, shine the towel and bring the boxers.

As I move painstakingly down the tree trunk, the black birds start returning, hundreds of them, and I get an uncomfortable feeling, like something sinister is watching me.

Why are there so many birds?

I hear a loud snap and look up to see a black explosion of wings. A moment later, the translucent sarcophagus comes barreling down the tree branches like a bobsled on a spiral staircase, heading straight for me. I force myself to look down for the first time, trying to gauge if I'm low enough to jump.

Before I have a chance to decide, I notice a flash of red moving through the ubiquitous green vegetation. There's an astronaut right out of *Space Odyssey: 2001* standing on the ridge watching me!

What the—

"Diego!"

I whip my head around at the sound of my name. There's a woman at the base of the tree staring up at me!

Isabel?

A damp towel drops over my head, and I lose my balance.

Shit!

My foot slips, pitching me backwards, and for a sickening moment, I watch the world slip by in slow-mo. The back of my head strikes a branch, pain shooting through my neck and back, and I tumble sideways into nothingness.

Chapter 2

Shannon: It's a Miracle

After I check all the readouts, I shut the cover of the pump house and attempt to secure the latch. The bulky gloves make it difficult to do simple tasks, but I'm used to it, and I don't rush.

If you don't take the time to do it right, how are you going to find the time to do it over?

I glance at my O_2 gauge and smile to myself. I'm always trying to beat my own record for oxygen consumption, and today is looking good.

Once I get everything locked back down, I radio Mindy that I've completed the task and start walking back around the fishpond to the main airlock.

"That's the last item on the list," she says in a bored voice.

Like I didn't know that already.

Mindy always complains that she has to sit next to the radio while I get to have all the fun, but I did score the highest of any D-1 on the biosuit training test, so I got the dangerous job.

Not like I'm bragging or anything.

Mom says bragging is a sign of insecurity, and that our actions should speak for themselves. Well, I've been going

Outside since I was knee-high to a ladybug, and I've never had an accident. Madders says that's because I'm careful and I follow the protocols, and he's the smartest man I know.

Discretion is the better part of valor.

"Come on," Mindy says. "Time to get your butt back inside. I'm trying to finish that stupid factoring polynomials homework, and I could use a little help."

We're not supposed to use the radio for anything except important communications, but Mindy always ignores stuff like that, and maybe that's why we're best friends. Like Mom says, we complement each other.

"Be there in a jiffy."

A huge flock of birds rises out of the forest to the west, and I stop for a minute and watch them, trying to estimate how many there are so I can record it in the log. And then I notice that the top of one pine tree is swaying. A lot.

That would have to be one giant bird to make a tree move like that.

The thought gives me the creeps, and it takes me a minute to decide what to do. I end up backtracking along the paved pathway to get a better look, and that's when I first see him.

And he's not wearing a biosuit.

"Uh, Mindy," I say, my hand shaking as I switch my suit radio back on. "You're not going to believe this, but there's someone climbing a tree out here."

"Uh-huh." I can hear her munching crackers back in the radio room, then there's a pause. "Did you just say what I think you did?"

"Yeah. There's a guy out here in a tree."

"What? Are you sure?"

"Pretty sure," I say. "And he's not wearing a suit. I'm putting it on visual now."

"Shannon, you've gone stark raving ma—" She makes a

squeal that causes feedback in my headset. "Holy shit, girl. I see him. He's not wearing a suit!"

"Duh. I just said that."

"Oh my god, he's not wearing *anything*!"

"Yeah," I say. "And why isn't he dead?"

"Shit, I don't know. Maybe he's holding his breath. What should we do?"

"Well, I've got two hours left on my suit," I say, watching the guy move along the branch, "so I'm going to check it out. Maybe you should go get someone."

"Wait there, Shannon. You're not supposed to do anything except simple maintenance when you're Outside. What if you poke a hole in your suit?"

"I won't."

"I'm getting your mom. Don't do anything until I get back!"

I switch off the camera and mic, then start climbing the embankment surrounding the pond, trying to keep my eyes on the man while being careful not to trip and fall. Everyone knows that biodome exos are dangerous, but unplanned ones are especially so.

Still, I know the drill—and I think this counts as an emergency.

But the suit is heavy and the incline steep, and after only a minute or two, I have to stop to catch my breath. I watch the man swing down to the next lower branch and edge toward the trunk. He's too far away to recognize, but he's definitely naked. I can see the dark patch of hair between his legs—but nothing more, um, interesting.

"Shannon Malia Kai!" Mom's voice comes over the radio. "You get back to the biodome this instant!"

"Hi, Mom. There's a man in a tree out here, and I'm investigating." I turn the camera back on. "Do you see him?"

"*Oka fefe.* He's naked!"

"Been there; done that," Mindy says.

For the first time, I notice something above the guy in the tree, and it must be something heavy, because the branch is bent way down. As I'm trying to figure out what it could be, the tree branch breaks and sends a whitish torpedo careening down toward the man.

He yells and scrambles out of the way, but his foot slips and he tumbles head first off the bouncing branch.

"That's not going to end well," Mindy says.

It takes the guy a long time to hit the ground.

"You turn straight around, Shannon Malia, and get your bottom back to the airlock this—"

I lower the volume in my suit and continue climbing. "I'm going after him."

"Shannon, stop!" Mom says, but I can barely hear her. "Madders is suiting up, and you need to wait until he gets there."

"That man could die in the fifteen minutes it'll take, Mom. Maybe I can help him."

"She does have a point," Mindy says.

"Shut it, Mindy," Mom says. "Let me think."

"You think while I climb," I say, still struggling uphill toward the fallen body. The loose dirt and rocks are slippery, and it's all I can do not to fall or tumble backward. I finally give up on trying to count the huge flocks of birds taking flight and focus on staying upright.

Damn biosuit weighs a metric ton. Why can't I just be Outside with an oxygen mask?

"Okay, baby," Mom says after I'm already halfway up the hill, "but leave the camera on. And don't touch him!"

"What's he going to do, Mom, infect me?"

Mindy laughs, but Mom cuts her off and addresses me.

"That's enough sass, young lady. Those who m-make m-mistakes Outside don't live to do it twice."

"Sorry, Mom," I say. "I won't touch anything."

"Unless he's got a knife stuck in his invisible clothes," Mindy says, "there's not much he could do short of biting her suit. And after a fall like that, he probably can't even open his mouth."

"And I'm following the protocol for exceptional situations," I add, glad to have Mindy running interference on her end.

"I don't like this one bit," Mom says. "Please be careful!"

There's a click, and Madders' voice comes through. "Glad to hear you're doing it by the book, Shannon."

"Hi, Madders. Thanks for the backup."

"You're welcome. But you should listen to your mother." His voice is calm, but firm.

Yeah, yeah.

"You know I always do," I say and turn back toward the biodome. There are four suits coming out of the airlock carrying a red first-aid kit and a stretcher. The suit in front looks up and waves, and I wave back.

"How much time do you have left on your tank?" he asks.

"Almost two hours. I was on course to break my O_2 record until Joe McNaked decided to go tree-diving."

He chuckles. "That's my girl." They start moving toward the pond. "Be there in a few minutes, so don't take any unnecessary risks. And leave your mic on."

"Ranger that." I continue up to the top of the ridge, trying not to breathe too loudly, then spot the man crumpled at the base of the huge tree. There's a lot of blood, and his arms and legs are bent in ways they shouldn't be.

"Can you see him?" I ask and turn the volume back up.

"Ouch," Mindy says.

"He fell at least five stories," Mom says. "And it probably killed him."

"Oh no! He can't be dead." I can't keep the disappointment out of my voice. It's not every day you find a naked man Outside.

"Yes, baby, I'm sorry," Mom says. "And that's close enough. The others are almost there."

"It's possible he's still alive, Mom. I'm going to check if he's breathing."

I pretend not to hear Mom cursing under her breath.

The huge branch that broke off is blocking my way, and the forest floor around the tree is thick with nasty-looking plants—some of which have thorns. I decide to climb up on some boulders and scoot across them on my bottom until I can get past the fallen branch. But my suit is getting heavier by the minute, and it's harder to get onto the rock than I expected. It takes me three attempts, and a lot of heavy breathing, before I manage it.

I start edging across the smooth boulder and then let out a startled yelp.

There's a rattlesnake coiled up next to my hand—its tail shaking and its head poised to strike.

"What's happening, Shannon?" Madders asks. "Are you all right?"

"Yes. Rattlesnake. Right next to my glove. I must have surprised it."

I can hear Mom's frightened cry.

"I'm going to pull my hand away really, really sl—"

The snake strikes, its fangs sinking into the fabric above my wrist, but missing my arm. I lift up my hand and fling the snake as far away as I can. A moment later, the breach alarm goes off in my suit.

"Shannon!" Mom shouts. "What's g-going on? Are you hurt?"

I glance at the green pressure indicator, knowing I only have a minute or so before the pressure drops and the virus gets in.

"I'm fine, Mom," I say and pull the small patch kit out of the quick-release pouch on my belt. "The snake punched two small holes in my sleeve, but it didn't bite me."

"*Oka fefe*, Madders, hurry!"

"We're almost there," he says. "Shannon, get a patch over that pronto."

"Already on it." I pull out the tab that releases the primer, but the patch slips out of my gloved hands and lands next to my thigh, primer-side up.

Thank goodness it didn't land the other way—or fall into the dirt.

Unfortunately, thin items are really hard to pick up with bulky gloves, and if I touch the epoxy, it will stick to my finger and be ruined.

For a second I consider using up the second patch, but if I don't manage to cover both bite holes with the first one, I'll need it—assuming I'm not dead by then.

"Shannon!" Mom yells, making me jump. "The p-pressure in your suit is dropping! What are you doing, baby? Hurry up! Oh my god, why did I let you go Outside?"

"You're not helping, Mom." I force down the urge to panic and place one hand next to the edge of the rock. I use the other to slide the sticky circle across the rock and into my palm, being careful not to tip it over or touch the epoxy.

"What's the holdup, Shannon?" Madders asks. "You need to get that patch on now!"

"Almost there." I flip the patch over onto my arm—covering both tiny holes in one shot—and let out a whoop. "Got it!"

"Holy shit," Mindy says. "What took you so long?"

"I dropped the patch." The alarm in my suit goes silent, but the pressure indicator is still in the red. "But everything's fine now." Ten long seconds later, it changes back to orange.

That was close.

I hear a click—probably Mom giving Madders an earful on a private channel—and rest for a minute, waiting for the suit pressure to go green. Once it does, I pick up a stick and use it to make sure there aren't any more snakes hiding in the rocks.

"I order you to stay where you are, Shannon." Mom sounds really mad, but if the mysterious tree man is still alive, she'll be too busy taking care of him to yell at me. "Madders needs to check your patch and make sure it's on properly."

"If it wasn't on properly," Mindy says, "she'd be croaking by now."

"Mindy!"

"She's right, Mom." I continue scooting across the smooth boulder. "And besides, I'm already there."

I slide carefully off the rock and land on my feet.

"Don't touch anything!" Mom says, her too-loud voice bouncing around inside my helmet.

"I won't, Mom." I check my suit pressure and air supply. Everything looks fine.

Jeepers, I hate being treated like a child.

I've never seen a guy naked before, and I can feel my heart pounding as I approach him. He's crumpled on his side with his back to me, so there are no boy parts visible.

I hope they're all still attached and functional.

"Can you move a little so we can see his, um, face," Mindy says.

I take a couple of steps closer, moving sideways so that I can see his front side. The ground is covered with translucent shards of ice—which is weird because there wasn't any ice on the pond today—and the rapidly-melting pieces crunch underneath my boots.

Maybe he knocked it off the tree branches when he fell?

The guy's longish, black hair is matted with blood, and his skin is a lot darker than mine, but not as brown as Madders' or Lucy's. I can't see his junk, as Mindy calls it, so I can't tell if he still has everything.

Not that it matters if he's dead, Shaz.

"His leg must be broken in six places," Mom says. "What was he doing up in that damn tree?"

"And more importantly," Mindy says. "Does he have a girlfriend?"

I hold still for a minute and focus on the naked guy's chest, watching for any movement.

"He's breathing!" Mindy and I say at the same time.

Oh my god, he's not dead. And I'm the one who found him.

"*Oka fefe*," Mom says, her voice full of disbelief. "Once Madders and Lucy get up there, you'll need to be extremely careful moving him. His back may be broken, and we don't want to do any more damage."

"I copy that," Lucy says. "Assuming I don't die before we get there. One little misstep and I'll be feeding the fish for the next decade. Lordy, I never signed up to go Daniel Boone-ing when I said yes to emergency medical duty this morning."

"Be careful, Miss Lucy!" I say.

"Bless your heart," she answers, her breathing audible.

"What should I do now, Mom?" I ask, flutters of excitement making my chest ache.

"Is it safe to move so we can see his face, baby?"

"Yeah, sure. Just a sec." I tramp around the tree, then stop and turn my camera back on the injured man.

There are broken bones sticking out of his arms and legs, and there's a bloody gash above his left ear, but his, um, *manroot* seems to be intact. Still, given all the stuff I've read, it does look kind of small and shriveled.

I'll have to ask Mindy about that.

I notice something bright orange in his hand. It's spattered with blood, and before anyone tells me not to, I use a dead leaf to pick it up.

"It's a real seashell!" I say, holding it up for the camera.

"Watch out!" Mom says. "Those spines look sharp!"

"Yep," I say and take a minute to admire the beautiful lines of orange and brown swirling around a milky white core.

If I put it up to my ear, will I be able to hear the ocean?

"Why would he be holding a seashell?" Mom asks.

"Because it's important to him," I say and place it carefully in a cargo pocket.

"Duh," Mindy says before Mom shushes her.

I turn back to the man. There's dark beard stubble covering his cheek and jaw, so he's definitely old enough to make babies, and he has nice hands with long fingers—and even some muscles in his chest.

Mindy squeals, and I know she's thinking the same thing I am.

Assuming he doesn't die, the dating options in the Bub just improved dramatically.

Madders walks up behind me, takes a quick look at the patch on my sleeve, and then rests his hand on my shoulder. "You did good, Shenanigans. I'm proud of you."

"Thanks, Madders. Just following protocol: Identify the problem, engineer a fix, and Bob's your uncle."

"Bloody right." He squeezes my shoulder, and we turn and watch Lucy and the others tramp up the hill. "We'll get him back to the biodome and see if your mom can fix him up good as new."

We turn back to the naked man, and I notice that all the ice has melted into the damp ground. "I don't recognize him, Madders. Do you?"

Madders shakes his head. "Except..." He steps closer. "Nah, couldn't be. He's definitely not from the Bub. Lani, you ever seen this guy before?"

"No," Mom says. "And just for the record, Miracle Man doesn't have a mask on."

"Nope," I say smiling, despite the fact that I just blew my oxygen consumption average for the next decade. "He's naked as a blue jay, and I call *chopes*."

Chapter 3

Diego: The Undead

I awaken inside a darkened room, and for a minute I wonder if I'm back in the Magic Kingdom. That underground city smelled like an old hunting lodge, but there's something else in the air here, some odor that tickles my memory.

I take a deep breath and wince.

I must not be dead or it wouldn't be this painful.

And then I remember where I am—or rather where I am not—and how I got here.

At least it's not the Jurassic.

I stare at the IV in my wrist, my heart racing.

So where the hell am I?

I try to sit up, but a sharp pain in my chest convinces me otherwise. I rest for a bit, forcing myself to calm down, then start again with wiggling my fingers and toes. My right arm and both my legs seem too heavy, and there's some sort of giant rubber band wrapped around my torso, but I don't seem to be missing any major body parts.

I take a more careful look around. I seem to be in a small hospital room. There's a small flat-panel display on one of the machines and digital locks on some of the cabinets—not something you'd expect to see twenty years in the past.

I'm in the wrong place and the wrong time?

If so, all the sacrifices and suffering, all the time away from Iz, will have been for nothing. Christ, I'm a time-traveling Robinson Crusoe stranded god-knows-where, while the world I left behind goes to hell in a hand-basket, taking the only woman I ever loved with it.

Screw-Up Nadales strikes again.

I close my eyes, waiting for the tidal wave of pain and loss to crush me, but instead of grief, I feel a numb emptiness.

Like I'm drugged.

The door opens, letting in a slat of light from the hallway, and a petite Asian woman walks in, long black hair pulled into a loose braid at the back of her neck. Her face is hidden in the shadows, but she looks to be in her thirties, wearing sensible shoes and casual clothes.

When she realizes that I'm awake, she brings up the lights. "Welcome back to the world of the living." Her voice is as silky as her straight black hair. She walks over to the bed, glances at the giant rubber band wrapped around my torso, and then turns to adjust my IV.

I stifle a gasp. One whole side of her face is a mass of raised and twisted flesh.

"I'm the one who glued you back together," she says. "My name's Lani."

I lie there like an idiot, staring in horror at what remains of her face.

She runs her fingertips across the scars and turns away. "It's been years since someone looked at me like that." She adjusts the papers on her clipboard, and when she turns back to me, there's a coldness in her eyes. "I'm sorry I startled you," she says. "I don't meet many new people." She shifts her weight. "I apologize if you find my appearance... d-distressing."

I stare at her, embarrassment keeping me mute, and then I look away.

Who or what did that to her?

"Do you speak English?" she asks, and when I don't respond, she adds, "*¿Habla Español? Sprichst du Deutsch?*" She makes an audible huff. "Damn, you don't look very Japanese, and I can't remember how to ask in French."

I force myself to look at her. "It's '*Parlez-vous français?*' And yes, I speak English and Spanish and *un peu français*—but *kein Deutsch*."

She purses her lips, a blush spreading over her porcelain skin. "I see."

Christ, she looks like she's never been out in the sun.

"As I said, I'm Dr. Kai, but most people just call me Lani. And you are mister..."

"Um, Crusoe. Diego Crusoe. Nice to meet you, doctor." I try to offer my right hand, but the cast extends from my shoulder down to my knuckles, and I only manage to wiggle my fingers. "Thanks for saving me."

She touches her fingertips to mine. "Nice to meet you, Mr. Crusoe. Thanks for dropping in."

"Please, call me Diego. All the people who save me do."

She laughs, a sound like a brook tumbling over round stones, and I get a weird feeling. Something about her is vaguely familiar, but I can't quite place it.

"Do you feel up to answering a few questions?" she asks. "I'm afraid the whole bubble is dying to hear your story, and if I don't throw them a bone, they'll just keep pestering me." She glances over at the half-open door. "You can go back to your homework now, girls. I'll let you know when he feels up to visitors."

Two teenage girls peek around the doorframe, smiling and waving their fingertips. They look to be sixteen or seventeen, and their complexions are also vampire white.

"I'm the one who found you," the blond girl says, blushing crimson. She's not much taller than Lani, but she's built like a gymnast and moves like one too, bouncing on the balls of her feet. Her straight, blond hair is pulled back in a ponytail and her eyes are glacier blue.

"But I helped," her friend adds, bumping shoulders with the blond. "I'm Mindy, and Miss Embarrassment here is Shannon."

I laugh. "Nice to meet you both."

If there are any teenage boys in vampire land, they must be lining up to ask these two out.

They giggle, and I can almost see the queue forming outside my door—especially for the shorter one: Her fine features, porcelain skin, and blond over blue are quite stunning.

"Thank you, girls," Lani says and shoos them out, shutting the door firmly. "Did I mention you're famous?"

"Indecent exposure?"

She chuckles. "In a manner of speaking. Do you know where you are?"

The absurdity of the question overwhelms me, and I start laughing.

Christ, I don't even know when *I am.*

My laugh turns into a coughing fit and pain shoots through my chest and shoulders. And then, I can't breathe. Lani rushes over to a cabinet and takes out a vial and a syringe.

"No more drugs," I manage to croak out, holding up my left hand. "I'm okay. Give me a minute."

She brings the items back with her, looking concerned.

I will myself to take slow breaths, and a few seconds later, it works. "Sorry." I give her a wan smile. "I'm sure it would look bad on your résumé if you spent all this time saving me, only to have me die of laughter."

"Very funny. Fortunately, I don't think you're going to expire any time soon."

"So, where am I? In a vampire hospital?"

She gives me a confused look.

"Everyone here has porcelain skin, you included."

One side of her mouth curves down. "Well, you're right about the hospital part. You took a bad fall. We weren't sure you were going to make it, but I think the worst is over now."

"Will I be able to walk again?"

"Eventually. But it will take some time."

"How much time?"

"That will depend on how hard you want to work. With injuries like yours, recovery can be slow and painful."

I glance down at my immobilized body and then raise one eyebrow. "So what's broken?"

"Probably easier to tell you what's not. You fell nearly twenty meters—over sixty feet. It's lucky a branch or two broke your fall."

"Right."

She points to my rubber-band-covered chest. "You fractured most of the ribs on your left side, but didn't puncture a lung— also very lucky." She runs her gaze over my lower half. "So everything internal is still in the right place, and everything external seems to be nominally functional."

"Good to know."

She brings her gaze back up to my face. "Your right shoulder was dislocated, and your back and neck were wrenched a bit, but they should be fine. You landed in a giant fern, which cushioned your fall somewhat, so thrice lucky."

"Yeah, I won the lottery."

She points to a bandage above my left ear, and I reach across my face and run my fingertips over it. "You took a good bump on your head there, but no fracture. Still, you may have headaches for a while. But if all goes well, we should have you good as new in a few months."

"A few months?" I lift my head and look over the expanse of blue fiberglass running from my right shoulder down to my knuckles.

"If Shannon hadn't seen you fall, you'd be dead, Mr. Crusoe. So in my book, you're the luckiest man alive."

"That's me."

"All things considered," she says, "I think you're doing smashing." One corner of her mouth curves up a millimeter, and given what's happened to her face, I take it for a smile.

Of all the doctors in the world, I get the one who likes word-play. I miss you, Iz.

"Thank you," I say. "And please give Shannon my thanks too."

She brushes my gratitude off with a wave of her hand. "Oh, you can thank her yourself in a day or two. She's been camped outside your room since they brought you back." She gets an amused look in her eyes. "And she's told all her friends that she has *chopes* on you, which I think is D-1 slang for dibs."

"Dibs in dee-won?"

She frowns, pulls up a chair, and sits down. "Where *are* you from?" She stares at the tanned skin on my arm and then looks up at me. "Obviously not here."

"Nope, not a drop of vampire blood in me."

"Good to know." She sets the unused syringe down on a tray by the bed. "D-1, decade one, or first decade: all the kids who were born within ten years of the Extinction. With only a few thousand people left in the gene pool, we had to do some planning."

My throat gets tight. "What are you talking about?"

She crosses her arms. "Children born in D-1 are strongly encouraged to find a mate from outside their extended family, D-2s from outside their bubble. We started doing it by generation, but that proved too complicated, so now it's just by birth year. By the time we get to D-3, I suspect we'll have to make the requirements even stricter."

I shift my weight, not really listening, and a pillow slips out.

She manages to catch it before it hits the floor, then spends a minute repositioning it behind my head and shoulders. When she's done, she places one hand on my good shoulder. "Better?"

"Yes, thank you. What year is it? And what caused the extinction?" I cough and then wince, and she reaches for the syringe, but I shake my head. "Maybe you could just start at the beginning and tell me everything?"

She's quiet for a minute, thinking, and then she sits back down in the chair. "You don't remember anything?"

I shake my head and a strand of my shoulder-length hair catches on my lip.

She reaches over and tucks it behind my ear. "You don't remember how you got in that tree? Where you came from? How long you'd been Outside?"

I know I'm a terrible liar, but I'm not ready to tell her the truth and end up in the loony bin. "No," I say. "I remember falling and hitting my head, but nothing else. I'm sorry."

"Well that's normal for a trauma patient. I would expect your memory to start coming back soon, though." She glances down at her hands folded in her lap, then back up at me, her eyes suddenly tired. "It's late, Diego, and you need to rest; so I'll answer those two questions, and then we'll call it a night, okay?" She's using her doctor voice now, gentle, but non-negotiable.

What is it that she doesn't want to tell me?

I nod and reach out for the glass of water by my bed, IV tube trailing. She leans across me and refills the glass, adjusts the straw, and then hands it to me. She lets her fingers remain around mine, waiting to make sure I've gripped the glass securely before letting go, and I feel a rush of warmth.

She watches me take a sip and then places the back of her hand over my forehead. "Your fever is down, but I'm going to leave the IV in for now."

I fall back into the pillow, suddenly exhausted. "Whatever you think," I say and shut my eyes. Her touch is cool and soft, and my thoughts drift back to the last time Iz and I made love, the memory compelling and traumatic at the same time.

"Is your memory returning?" Her voice startles me.

"No. I was just enjoying your touch," I say and smile, meaning it. "It's been a long time."

She takes her hand away. "The year is 2048, Diego."

The smile slips off my face and shatters into sharp little pieces on the floor.

Shit. That's almost twenty years in the future.

There's a flutter of panic in my chest, but it doesn't get any traction, and a minute later it disappears, leaving me feeling disoriented.

I clear my throat. "And what is a bubble?"

"You're in one right now: the Kirk Biodome, also known as the Bub. We're a few miles northeast of where the Powers military base used to be."

So I'm still in Colorado, twenty-odd years in the future.

"Why are we in a biodome?"

She sighs. "This one was built eighteen years ago. It was the first of its kind and was sealed a few hours after the Doomsday Virus was reported in the area."

"And you've been inside ever since? You're stuck in here?"

"Yes." She stands up, checks my IV again, and adjusts the flow.

"What are you giving me?" My voice has an edge, and the question comes out as more of an accusation.

"Mainly fluids and some nourishment. Most people find it difficult to eat and d-drink while they're unconscious." She doesn't look at me.

I stare at the colorless liquid dripping into my vein. "What else?"

"Nothing out of the ordinary, Diego. Painkillers—and a mild antidepressant."

I open my mouth to protest, but she doesn't let me.

"You have over nineteen fractures, including five in one leg. If I wasn't giving you medication, you'd be comatose with pain."

I take a minute to think about it. There do seem to be monsters sloshing around in the back of my head, but I can't seem to hold on to them long enough to feel any trepidation.

"Now that you're awake," she says, "I'll give you control of the painkiller, and if you would prefer, I'll have Lucy stop the antidepressant."

"Thank you. Yes." I force myself to look away from the IV. "Please go on. You were telling me about the bubble."

She glances at her watch, but obliges. "There are eighty-three biodomes left in the Americas, 317 worldwide. Somewhere around 100,000 people survived the initial outbreak, but a number of biodomes weren't finished and some that *were* finished didn't seal properly." She slides the chair back against the wall and then stands by my bed, her arms folded across her chest. "By the end of the year, fewer than 40,000 people were still alive."

"In the whole world?"

"Yes. The vast majority are in biodomes in the US, Europe, Japan, and Australia, but the Russians have some giant underground city in the Urals too. We don't have much contact with them, given all the finger pointing that went on after the nuke was launched, so we don't have an exact count. The good news is most of the bubbles in the US were built to house 300 people, but the average is down below a hundred now, so we've plenty of room to grow."

"Christ. That red-headed kid's predictions were correct."

"What predictions?"

I can feel sweat breaking out underneath my myriad casts. "Uh, you know, all those doomsayers from the last century warning about mankind doing himself in with nukes or bioweapons."

"Right," she says. "Okay, lights out. I'll be back in the morning to check on you."

"How many people survived here?"

"You mean the United States?" She glances at me, and I nod. "Somewhere around seven thousand, the majority in bubbles built in moderate climates along the coasts. As far as I know, this is the only one built at such a high altitude and so close to the mountains."

For the second time I sense something familiar about her, but I can't seem to grab it. "We're in Colorado?"

"Yep. Next closest biodome is west of the Rockies near Salt Lake." She gives me a skeptical look. "Are you starting to remember things?"

I shake my head, and then it comes to me. "You're the street kid! The one who helped me save Isabel from the fire. I watched you break into that jewelry store, and then I convinced you and your friends to help me smash the kitten's window in the hotel."

She gives me a blank look.

"You saved all the animals. Don't you remember? *War and Peace*—and Tolstoy? And goddamn Lucky?"

"I'm sorry, but I don't know what you're talking about." A worried look crosses her face. "Are you feeling disoriented?"

I stare at her, certain that I'm right.

Only in this universe it must have played out differently.

"Maybe a little," I say. "It was a long time ago, and I guess I was hoping you might know something about..." I shrug. "Thanks again for saving my life, Dr. Kai."

"Please call me Lani. And, once again, you're welcome." She looks at me for a minute, making some sort of decision. "But to be completely honest, there's a more selfish reason."

I give her the Spock eyebrow.

She turns away and fills up my water glass again. Then she picks up her clipboard, walks over to the door, and places her hand over the light switch. "In the nearly twenty years since Doomsday hit, you're the only human being who has been Outside unprotected and lived to tell about it."

I glance down at my body. "How do you know I'm not infected?"

"Everyone else died in a matter of minutes."

"Shit. That sounds horrible."

"It was." She dims the lights. "Good night, Robinson Crusoe. Sleep well." She shuts the door, and I hear the clipboard swinging on the hook outside.

One, two, three...

A split second later, I'm asleep.

Chapter 4

Lani: Lost and Found

After I make sure that Shannon is settled in for the night at Mindy's, I hurry back over to the clinic, a dark shadow hanging over me. The biodome is out of pain meds, and Miracle Man is going to have a long night ahead of him. A scavenging party went out over a week ago, and they should have been back by now, but every year they have to go farther, and every year they return with less.

What are we going to do when all the medicine is gone?

"Worry about the things you can control," I say to myself, "and let the rest go."

There's a blizzard raging Outside tonight, and the aging biodome is moaning and creaking under the added force of the storm. Madders is out with the foraging party, but he assured me before he left that the damaged west wall would hold until replacement parts could be found and installed.

But he's not here tonight if something goes wrong...

I stop and listen to the wind yanking on the loose piece of wall in sector four, slamming it against the weakened framework over and over. At least with the wind, we don't have to worry about the weight of the snow on the roof—assuming the storm doesn't tear the whole thing down tonight.

I hold my breath and count to ten, checking for the slight breeze that signals a breach in the dome.

The air is cold and still.

I offer up a plea to the mountain gods to keep those who are Outside safe and those who are inside alive for another night.

And then I force myself to keep walking, unable to shake the ominous feeling that our time is running out.

"How's he doing?" I ask as I enter the clinic.

Lucy is sitting at the nurses' station, finishing the drug inventory, a traditional nurse's hat pinned in her hair. Her face is drawn and tired, and I know the answer before she says a word.

"Well, doc, I've been giving him the over-the-counter drugs just like you said, but his fever is up, and he's in a lot of pain. He won't eat or drink, and he's thrashing around so bad the IV won't stay in."

"Damn."

She gives me a worried look. "And his demons are back."

It's been a long time since I had to watch someone suffer, and the thought brings up acid in the back of my throat. "I'll stay with him tonight," I say, forcing down images of anguished children crying out for their dead parents. "Go home and get some rest."

"But you were up last night!" she says, crossing her arms. "And the last thing we need is for our only doctor to get si—"

"I'll be fine, Lucy. See you in the morning."

She looks like she's going to protest, but exhaustion wins out. "Yes, ma'am. The tallies for everything we have left are right here." She tucks a sheet of paper back into the box with the few remaining prescription meds. "Plenty of anti-malarial tablets should there be a sudden upswing in the mosquito population."

I force a smile. "At least that's one thing we don't have to worry about."

"Praise the Lord."

"I'll lock everything back up for you."

She nods and starts collecting her things. "I may stop by the radio room and see if they have an update on the foraging party. We could sure use those drugs—and Becky's help. Wake me up if you need relievin'? I ain't slept well since Emmett passed, so it's no bother."

"Thank you, Lucy, I will. And could you pass on an evacuation order for sector four, please? Tell them I said it's just a precaution. No need to panic people, but if the storm gets worse, and that weakened strut gives out, we won't have enough masks for everyone."

She gives me a tired smile. "They issued the order thirty minutes ago, and I suspect the bulkheads are being sealed even as we speak. They're calling it a drill, but I don't think anyone was fooled."

"Good. Shannon is staying with Mindy, so let the council know our place is available if someone needs it?"

"Will do." She ambles toward the door. "See you first thing in the morning, doc, and good luck."

"Thanks, Lucy. Try to get some sleep."

I tiptoe down the hall to Miracle Man's room and push the door open a crack.

Lucy has left a small light on, and I can see Diego tossing about on the bed, the white plaster casts on his arms and legs leaving afterimages in the dim light.

It was twenty years ago that I lay in a similar bed, begging them to let me die. I was in the ICU when the bomb went off, the blast taking out a huge section of the biodome wall in sector four. The hospital had to be evacuated, and I was suddenly one among hundreds who had been maimed or burned by the explosion or the resulting fire. Due to my compromised immune system—or maybe my connection to David—I had been given one of only a handful of private rooms in this makeshift clinic, but I could still hear the cries of the others out in the hallway, begging for water or morphine or death.

No matter how hard I try to erase that memory, I can still see Bella staring at me, her face bathed in the flickering shadows of the emergency lamps.

She didn't even bother to come into the room. "She'll live," she said to no one in particular and added, "the ungrateful tramp." I remember watching the celebrated doctor step back through the doorway, her bony white hand grabbing Lucy's arm. "Change the bandages, but don't give her any more pain meds. We're going to need them for later."

She was right, of course.

"No," Diego calls out, banging his cast against the bedrail. "Iz, please. Don't leave me!"

I take a clean washcloth out of the drawer, get it damp, and then sit down in the chair by Diego's bed, wishing there was more I could do.

Who are you, and why are you here?

"Why did I wait so long?" His voice is weak, sobs slipping out around his labored words. "I need you, hun. Please don't die!"

"Shh," I say, dabbing at his feverish face. "I'm here now."

He moans, pain twisting up his handsome face. "Oh god, not the babies—they're so beautiful, so perfect—little Soleil's lovely eyes and Lucas' tiny hands. How could they be dead, Isabel?"

I stroke his cheek with the back of my hand. "Everything is going to be okay."

"No!" He struggles against the twisted sheets, his clothes drenched with sweat and his hair matted against his face.

"Shh," I say, placing the cool washcloth across his forehead. "Rest now."

He grabs my wrist, his palm hot and sticky. "Don't leave me, Iz!"

"I won't. Go to sleep." I use my other hand to sweep the tangled hair back from his tortured face. "I'll be right here when you wake up."

He sighs and then shuts his eyes, his hand still gripping my wrist. "I tried to get back to you, Iz. But they wouldn't let me go."

"I know you did. Go to sleep, Diego."

He entwines his fingers with mine, holding my hand against his feverish cheek. "You have to get to Dave. He can save you, Iz. Please. You need to leave now."

I kiss him on the forehead and then put my head down next to his shoulder. "I did, Diego. I made it inside the biodome. We're both safe now."

He turns his head and looks at me, his eyes damp. "I love you, Iz."

"Shh. Go to sleep. Everything will be better in the morning."

He nods and his eyes flicker shut.

I sit in the darkness, the moans of the aging biodome like my own sobs of despair.

The hours pass, his feverish body wracked with tremors one minute and shuddering with chills the next. I try to give him more medication, but he refuses to let go of my hand, and I eventually give up and rest there next to him, both of us waiting for the storm to pass, both of us trying to believe that everything is going to be all right.

Chapter 5

Diego: Angels & Demons

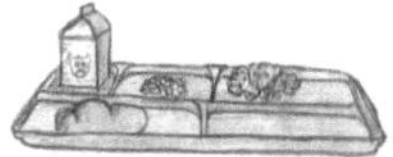

There's a soft knock on the door, and I rush to dry my face.

Lani walks in, clipboard in hand. "Good morning." Her voice is chipper, but her eyes get big when she notices that I've been crying. She strides over to the window and busies herself opening the blinds while I attempt to regain control.

"I'm afraid the strongest painkiller we have left is aspirin," she says. "But we do have plenty." She holds up a small bottle of white pills, but I shake my head.

Maybe it would help with the pain in my body, but there's nothing to be done about the pain in my heart. Isabel is dead, and everything I care about is gone. I walked away from the only woman I ever loved because I was stupid enough to think I could save her. She begged me not to go, not to abandon her, but I had to be the hero. In the end, all I did was seal her death warrant.

God, I'm tired of pretending to have something to live for.

I've been in this bed for thirteen days and nights, enough time to have a good long think about my life, and it's pretty hard to come up with any future that doesn't hold more suffering.

Lani comes over to my bed, her expression unreadable. "I apologize for barging in so early, but Lucy is concerned about you, and when Lucy worries, I take it seriously." She glances at my face and then the pillow. "I'll ask her to bring in some tissues. I think we can spare a box."

I attempt to tell her I don't want any more of her charity, but nothing comes out except a pathetic choking sound.

She pushes the hair back from my face and pulls an errant strand from between my lips. "I think you should take some of the aspirin. It will help with the pain."

I look away, still unable to speak.

She lifts her hand and runs a finger down her clipboard. "We do have a few more antidepressants. Would you like me to get you one?"

I find my voice. "No. I told you, I don't want any more happy drugs."

She pulls a chair over from the corner and then sits down. "Okay. I can't say I blame you. If you want to get better, at some point you'll have to face reality, however painful that might be."

I shut my eyes. "I don't want to get better. I want to die."

A scene from *The Andromeda Strain* runs through my head: Tumbleweeds blow across a desolate one-lane highway leading into an isolated town. It's late summer, and the scene is dusty and hot. Dogs lie sprawled on the parched lawns and cats on threadbare porch swings, their mouths hanging open in grotesque attempts to breathe the poisoned air. The camera pans out. Dead bodies are everywhere: men slumped against steering wheels, children crumpled next to empty park swings, women collapsed on the worn parquet tile of a lifeless shop. The camera zooms in on a single face, and Isabel's dead eyes stare back at me.

"I think it might help to talk about it, Diego." She places her hand on my good arm.

I stare at her, forcing down angry and hurtful words.

"Maybe I can help?" Her voice is barely audible, but my anguish and despair are too much, and the floodgates spill open.

"Everyone I love is gone, and you think I fucking want to talk about it? In my world, there are no biodomes, which means no survivors." I whack the breakfast tray next to my bed and dishes full of uneaten food clatter to the floor. "Isabel is dead. They're all dead. Everyone except me is feeding the worms, doc. I was the one who was supposed to change things, but I failed."

She takes a deep breath, then stands and walks around the bed.

"My world is dead and buried," I say to her empty chair. "I should be too."

I watch her pick up the fallen items and place them back on the tray. Without a glance at me, she strides across the room, takes a towel out of the dirty laundry bin, and then wipes up the mess on the floor. She rinses the towel out in the sink, scoops the food out of the drain, and tosses it in the trash.

I swallow hard, feeling like a complete asshole.

"Survivor's guilt is a very common reaction to what you've been through. If you weren't feeling it, I'd be *more* w-worried." She slides one fingertip across the scars running down her face. "I know it doesn't make you feel any better, but I know what you're going through, and with time, you'll heal."

I let out a disbelieving huff, and her eyes narrow into a frown.

"You may not be the same person as before," she says. "But you still have a life worth living. And I'll be damned if I'm going to let you throw it away because of self-pity."

I look more carefully at her. The damaged skin covers most of the right side of her face, continuing down her neck and under her blouse. It doesn't touch her eye, but clips the edge of her lips, rising all the way up into her straight black hair.

She waits for me to stop staring, her face blank. "Are you done?"

I feel the righteous anger inside me fizzle and die. "Yeah." I look down at my own injuries, all of which are healing, thanks to her. "I'm sorry about whatever happened to you."

"Thank you. I'm sorry about what happened to you too."

"Great. So now we know everyone is sorry. How about we throw a party?"

She sits on the edge of my bed and places her hand on mine. "I don't know how you managed to survive, or if there are more people like you, but the fact that we found you Outside has given everyone hope." She glances down at our hands and then back up at me. "Are there others like you? Others with a natural immunity?"

"Natural immunity?" I stare at her. "I don't know."

"There have always been rumors, people who claimed to have seen lights Outside at night, or members of foraging parties who caught glimpses of what they thought were ragged children."

I shake my head, unable to meet her eyes.

"Is that who you are, one of the survivors?"

I look up "No."

She opens her mouth to ask another question, but stops and looks away. I toy with the idea of asking about her scars, but I don't know if I can stand to hear about any more horrors.

I shift my cast-covered legs, and she reaches down to help. "Can I get you something?"

"Information on this fishbowl, and the low-down on how you became vampires?"

"A bit of a mixed metaphor," she says. "But I'll see about getting you a laptop so you can connect to our local net and purchase a silver cross and garlic."

"Thank you."

She makes a note on her clipboard and then looks back at me. "Anything else?"

"You said there are only a few thousand survivors. Is there a registry somewhere of the people who made it?" I tell myself it's a false hope, but still the words spill out. "Is there a way to find out what happened to a specific individual?"

She takes a deep breath and lets it out slowly. "Yes. But as I told you, very few people got to the biodomes in time. The chances that any one person survived are less than one—"

"—in eight billion."

She stands up and walks down to the foot of my bed, straightening out the sheets over my useless legs. "The Salt Lake Biodome has records from before, and they have information on everyone who survived. They also collect and collate the yearly census data, so if they find a living relative, they can tell you what biodome he or she is in."

She lifts the sheet off one foot and gently checks my toes. "Unfortunately, they don't keep that information on a computer. Back in the day, some crackpot started preaching that Doomsday was a computer virus that mutated into a real one, and believe it or not, a few nuts bought it." She examines my other foot. "They don't use any technology, so the search will require examining thousands of p-paper documents." She looks up. "It could take months to get an answer."

"I'm not going anywhere."

"Right." She replaces the sheet and straightens it again. "Your legs are healing nicely. Good circulation in your toes." She pulls a blank sheet of paper off her clipboard and hands it to me. "I'll need names and birth dates. If you have their last known locations, that may help too." She shifts her weight. "And as I said, it takes weeks to research a *single* name."

"Will two names be too many?"

"No," she says, her shoulders relaxing. "Two will be fine."

She walks back to the chair and perches on the edge, her eyes down. "Still..."

"Thank you, Lani."

She looks up when I say her name, and then she hands me a pen. "Who are you? Really."

"A man who should be dead." I take the offered items. "Who are you?"

Her voice is a whisper. "A woman who should be dead."

She stands and walks to the door, sliding the empty chair back against the wall as she goes. "We need you, Diego. We need you to help us figure out how to go back Outside." She leans against the doorframe. "I know you're angry about things, but there's not a lot of time to wallow in regrets. The biodomes were all built over two decades ago, and they were meant to be a short-term solution. We're rapidly running out of ideas, resources, and time."

She waves her hand in the air. "The air scrubbers are slowly failing. That's the amine you can smell. And the seals have begun to harden and crack. When they fail, the bubble will have to be abandoned, and we won't be able to take all the hospital equipment with us. Medical care will fall backward a hundred years, perhaps more." She glances out the door. "And Shannon may never have a chance to grow up and have children."

"Thanks for being so cheerful. I feel better already."

One corner of her mouth curves up. "I'll be back after rounds this afternoon to check on you—and pick up that list."

"Thank you, doctor."

She nods and starts to shut the door, then opens it again. "Oh, and I told Shannon she could bring you lunch. Like I said, you're a celebrity, and I think it's time you step up to the plate."

She shuts the door without meeting my gaze.

"Nothing like being signed up to save the whole goddamn world..."

Again. Christ.

∞

I buzz the day nurse, and she responds a microsecond later. "Yes, Mr. Crusoe?"

"Lucy, you're a paragon of virtue. Thank you for being concerned about me and my mental health."

"Y'all both are welcome. You were pretty tore up when we brought you in, everything catty-wompus and all. Lordy, I wish there was more I could do."

"There is one thing," I say.

"Shoot."

"Would it be possible to get some clothes and maybe a rubber-band to tie back my hair, please? I think my extended stint wallowing in self-pity and smelly pajamas is over."

"I'll see what I can find, Mr. Crusoe." There's a smile in her voice. "Will shorts and a T-shirt do or were you fixin' to get a lick more gussied up?"

"Shorts would be wonderful, thank you."

"I could probably arrange for a haircut, if that'd suit you?"

"That's very kind of you, Lucy, but I think I'll wait for now. I know it sounds silly, but it's my only connection to where I came from—the past I've lost—and until I get things sorted here, I need that bond."

"I understand perfectly."

∞

Two hours and one embarrassing sponge bath later, Lucy helps me get dressed, combs out my hair and ties it back with a strip of cloth. "Mm-mm, if you aren't just healing up nicely." She holds the mirror while I shave, then props me up with pillows on the newly changed bed.

I can't bend either of my legs, so a wheelchair is impractical for now, but it does feel great to be sitting up.

Lucy finishes cleaning up and then fluffs up an extra pillow and stuffs it behind my lower back. She steps back and looks at me. "I didn't realize there was such a handsome man under all that hair."

I laugh. "Thanks for rediscovering me."

She smiles and pats the maroon pillbox hat she's wearing today. "Dern tootin'. Anything else?"

"No, but I do have a question. About Lani."

Her smile disappears. "Now don't you go bothering our Lani. That woman has seen more evil than any one person should have to endure. And if you want to know about her accident, you'll have to ask her yourself. But I do know it dern near killed her—in more ways than one."

I swallow and glance down at Lani's handiwork, feeling like a self-centered ass.

"In any case," she adds. "It happened a long time ago, and maybe she wants to leave it be, if you get my drift?"

"Yeah," I say. "Thanks."

She squeezes my good shoulder. "Be sure to ask the doc about your legs. I think they've healed up enough to switch over to removable splints, and I imagine it would be nice to take a proper shower and get yourself out of this hospital room on occasion."

I take her hand and kiss it. "Thanks, Lucy. You're an angel."

She laughs. "Lordy, don't let Shannon see you do that. She's planning to card you the instant doc gives her the green light."

"Card me?"

"I'll let Shannon answer that one," Lucy says. "*She's* your real guardian angel—and she should be bounding in any minute."

Chapter 6

Shannon: Finders, Keepers

"Hey, Shaz. What are you doing here so early?" Mindy plops down next to me in the cafeteria and uses her algebra book to shove my lunch tray out of the way.

"Whoa," I say and pull my plate back in front of me. "I can't help with math now. I'm taking Mr. C his lunch today!"

"No way!"

"Yes way. I found him, so I get first *chopes* at him."

"Can I come?"

"Nope. Mom says one visitor a day until further notice."

"Shit. You get to have all the fun." She snags the cookie off my tray. "Are you going to ask him?"

We stare at each other for a second, and then I nod.

She lets out a squeal and glances around self-consciously. The cafeteria is getting busy, but we're still the only ones at this table.

"Remember when you asked me about boy parts?" she says, scooting closer to me. "Well take a look at these hunks in the buff."

"Hunks in the buff?"

"OMG, Shaz, you are so mank." She tosses her hair back over her shoulder in that condescending way she has and starts flipping through the algebra book. "*Hunks* are guys with lots of muscles, and *in the buff* means they don't have any clothes on." She stops at a picture tucked inside the textbook.

"Oh, right." I sneak a peek at the photo and almost choke on my rice and beans. "Wow. I didn't know their, um, *thing* could get that big."

"It's a penis, Shannon. And the men just pump them up for the photos." She runs her fingertip down the model's bare chest and then flips the thin magazine page over.

The guy on the other side is even bigger.

"Yikes."

"Yeah," she says. "I think his got over-inflated. My sister says they kept people off-camera to blow them up between shots. But if you put too much air in a penis, it can explode."

"Ouch."

"Defo." She gives me a knowing look. "That's probably what happened to Mr. C."

"His penis popped?"

"Yep. Poor guy. And it can take a long time to heal. And once it does, he can't inflate it by himself. Sis says it helps if you put your hand on it when it's deflated to show the guy you don't mind that he's burst. You know, build up his self-confidence a bit."

"Gotcha." I glance at the clock. "Oh my gosh, I need to go. Can we look at the hunks of buff again this afternoon?"

"Sure thing." She puts the book back in her pack. "But you have to tell me *everything* about Mr. C."

"Cross my heart and hope to croak." I get up and take my dishes to the soapy bin, Mindy tagging along behind me.

"Die, Shaz. It's *hope to die*."

"What?" Mr. Miller sees me and waves me back to pick up Mr. C's lunch tray.

"Never mind," Mindy says, heading over to sit with the boys. "See you this afternoon!"

∞

I walk through the open door carrying Mr. C's lunch tray, my heart beating a meter a minute.

"And here she is now," Miss Lucy says like I'm Miss America or something.

"Hi, Mr. C," I say, waving with my fingertips. "Nice to see you again."

"The pleasure is mine, Shannon." The way he says my name with that dreamy foreign accent makes me melt. "And thanks for saving me."

"Sure thing," I say, feeling all fluttery inside. "It's not every day you get to see a naked man fall out of a tree." I bat my eyelashes at him just like Scarlett does to Rhett. "Actually, I felt pretty lucky to be there."

Miss Lucy rolls her eyes, collects the dirty laundry, and then walks to the door, shaking her head the whole way. "You two have a nice little chat." She nods at me and then winks at Mr. C —like they have some sort of secret between them. "Buzz if you need something."

"Right-oh," Mr. C says.

I set the tray down by his bed and take my first good look at the guy everyone calls Miracle Man. I can see why Mom thinks he's handsome. His long hair is pulled back in a ponytail just like all the buff guys on Mindy's books, and he has really cute lips—like you have to kiss them or you're going to die of longing.

"Is it okay if I call you Mr. C?" I say, feeling a little warm. "Mom said to be sure to ask."

He laughs, deep and sexy, and it reminds me of that Zorro guy Mindy is so hot on.

She's going to be so jealous.

"Mr. C is fine," he says, still smiling. "Who's your very smart mom?"

"Dr. Kai, silly. Even though she doesn't have a parchment from a famous university, she's the best doctor this side of C-Bay —*and* she's my mother."

"Well if you ask me, diplomas are overrated. Thanks for bringing my lunch, Shannon. I hope you brought enough for two?"

"Oh no," I say, feeling a lump form in my throat. "I... couldn't. And besides, I already ate." I take the napkin off the tray and place it across his lap, making sure I brush my hand against his boy parts like Mindy suggested. "Mom says you need lots of protein, and the only way to get enough is to eat fowls."

"Fowls?"

"Yeah, you know, birds." I pull down the legs of the tray, smooth out the sheets over his boy parts, and set the whole thing in front of him. "Um, would you like me to stay and keep you company?"

He stares at me, his eyes big, and I'm pretty sure he must have gotten popped like the guy in Mindy's magazine.

"Uh, sure. That's very kind of you to offer."

I watch him take a bite of the bird, trying not to make a face. "So. How's the hen?" I grab a chair and sit down next to him.

"The hen?"

I nod at his lunch.

"Oh, that hen. It's good, thanks. Where I come from we call it chicken."

"Oops," I giggle, feeling a little awkward. "I hope you don't think I'm a limbo."

He raises one eyebrow in a way that is totally hot, and I make a mental note to tell Mindy about it. "Limbo?" he asks.

Damn, I must have gotten it wrong.

"You know," I say, "a limbo: just some unintelligent, mank girl who says dumb stuff to impress guys."

"Ah." He stifles a smile. "I think the word's *bimbo*." For a second, I feel really embarrassed, but then he adds, "Which you are clearly not. If I had to guess, I'd say you're very smart *and* very well-mannered—and not the least bit mank, whatever that is."

All the women in the romance books slide their hands across their hips when someone gives them a compliment, so I try it. He gives me a strange look, so I don't know if it worked.

"Uh..." he says. "Where do you keep the hens?"

"Here in the bubble, of course. Otherwise they'd run away." He says some of the strangest things. "We use the eggs mostly, but this one broke a wing and wouldn't stop squawking." I make a clicking noise and slice my finger across my neck.

"Yeow. I'll do my best not to squawk."

I giggle again and scoot my chair closer. "You're funny, Mr. C." I glance at his tray, hoping he won't be offended by my next question. "Mom says you're not from around here. Is that why you wear your hair so long?"

"You could say that."

"Mom and Miss Lucy think you should cut it." I look up into his dreamy brown eyes. "But I like it long."

He looks a bit embarrassed. "Thank you."

"And Mom wants to know if you have any kids."

He takes a drink of water. "You can tell her no, I don't."

I hop up and refill his water glass, happy to have something to do. "Well, I don't want to sound pushy or anything, but I did find you, and I wanted to ask you before anyone else does."

"Ask me what, Shannon?"

I sit on the very edge of the chair and lift my chest, just like Mindy says to do to show off my cleavage. "I was wondering if you'd consider signing my card." I'm too nervous to meet his eyes, so I pretend to look out the window.

"Ah." His tone is amused, and I jerk my head back in time to see his gaze leave my chest.

Obviously he thinks you're too young and stupid to be good at inflating anything.

"Does that mean you're carding me?" he asks.

I nod and flop back into the chair. "So what do you say?"

"I'm sorry, Shannon, but I'm not sure what that means. Lucy had mentioned something about it, but you arrived before she could explain everything."

"Oh." I try not to look disappointed. "Miss Lucy is *way* too old to have kids, and If *she* tried to card you, then it's way worse than Mindy and I thought. Mom wouldn't let me in until today, and I knew you'd be hot."

"Well, no, actually, I'm not carded—or hot, for that matter. Lucy just mentioned it to me, but she didn't get around to finishing."

"It means you agree to mix your DNA with mine so I can have your babies. Once I'm twenty-one, of course, but Mom says I should wait until I'm twenty-five."

He laughs, and my chest gets tight.

"What's so funny?"

"I'm sorry, Shannon. It's just that you surprised me." He pats my leg. "But you should definitely wait until you're twenty-five to have kids."

I can barely breathe my heart is beating so fast. "But I'm allowed to practice once I turn eighteen, and my birthday's only a couple months away." I bite my lip and then remember that Mom told me not to do that. "You don't have to sign my card right now—that's only if you want to make a baby with me. But we could practice just for fun. Maybe I can help blow your boy parts back up."

He gulps.

"Assuming you want me to," I add, feeling a little light-headed.

"Wow," he says. "Seventeen, going on eighteen. And you're obviously smart *and* pretty." He takes another bite of the hen and rice. "I'm very flattered, Shannon, and I'm sure, uh, practicing with you would be quite enjoyable."

Yes!

"But, I'm way too old for you."

I stand up. "You are not. Mom says you're thirty-five, and that gives you ten more years to have sex."

He looks up at me, the corner of his mouth twitching. "I'm closer to forty, actually, but that's beside the point. You should practice with someone your own age."

"That would be silly, Mr. C. The boys around here don't know anything!" I cross my arms. "I know you think I'm just an inexperienced kid. But, I'm not. I'm top of my class in school, and I'm healthy and strong. And lots of guys have asked to sign my card—Jake Wilson did yesterday, and Tommy Mueller did last month *and* last week, and he's twenty-six."

"Wow."

I pick up his lunch tray and set it on my chair. "And I'm going to *be* somebody someday. Mom doesn't believe me, but I'm working on a project to fix the rebreathers so people can go Outside without biosuits." I give him a defiant look. "And I also happen to know all about men. Just ask Mindy."

He lifts his eyebrow again. "I'm sure you do, Shannon, and I bet there are lots of guys who would kill to practice with you, but I..." He exhales.

You're losing him, Shaz. What would Mindy do?

I sit down on the edge of his bed and slide my hand up his

thigh. "You don't have to say yes right away." I move my finger-tips closer to his boy parts. "Maybe we could practice once, and if you don't like it, then we could stop?" I gaze up into his face and bat my eyelashes again.

He swallows. "Uh, well, perhaps we should just start with being friends?"

I lift my shoulder and toss my hair just like Marilyn Monroe does. "Or I could, you know, do stuff for you until you get stronger." I lick my top lip and move my hand closer to his boy parts.

Miss Lucy walks in the door carrying a stack of clean clothes, and I slip my hand back into my own lap. She glances at the clock. "Isn't it time you skedaddled to class, Shannon?"

"Sure thing, Miss Lucy. And I love your hat." She wears a different hat every day, and I know she's a little vain about them.

"This ol' thing? Lord, what I wouldn't give to go hat shopping one last time before I die." She tucks the clothes in a cabinet, her back to us. "I'll return the tray for you, Shannon, but you best be getting off."

I stare at Mr. C, trying to decide if I should do it.

Now or never.

I lean forward and kiss him hard on the mouth. He lets out a startled gasp, and I move my mouth next to his good ear. "Don't worry," I whisper. "We'll get your penis re-inflated. Pinkie promise!" I hop off the bed.

"Pinkie promise?" His eyes are huge.

He definitely has the hots for me. I can tell.

He glances at Miss Lucy and then back at me, looking a bit disoriented. "Thanks for bringing me lunch, Shannon."

"You're welcome, Mr. C." But as I'm bounding toward the door, I get this great idea. "Hey..."

He looks over at me, a goofy expression on his face—like he's madly in love.

"Mindy's mom Becky is having her birthday today, and a bunch of us are going to watch the movie *Shrek* to celebrate. We could bring it over here, if you like." I bite my lip, hoping I'm not overstepping my bounds. "So you and Miss Lucy could watch, too."

Miss Lucy brings her finger to her lips. "We'll have to check with the doc about all those visitors, but I think it's a wonderful idea. I bet we could even round up some popcorn. What do you say, Mr. C?"

He hesitates, and Miss Lucy gives him a *Don't be a party-pooper!* look.

"Please?" I say, putting on my best pout.

He laughs. "Okay, okay. I can't fight the both of you. I'd love to."

"Woohoo!" I clap my hands together.

"Off you go now," Miss Lucy says. "Your mother will skin us both if you're late for class."

"See you tonight, Mr. C!" I blow him a kiss and race off to tell Mindy everything.

Chapter 7

Lani: Guys & Dolls

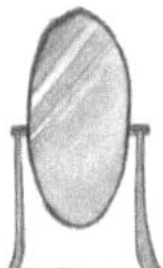

I force myself to look at the mangled face in the mirror, my eyes tracing the grotesque flesh that runs from above my right ear, across my cheek and neck, down my torso to the point of my hip. The burn scars are raised and twisted, garish splotches of pink with gray tentacles radiating out from the scarred flesh, making me look like some rotting zombie.

He stared at me like I was some sort of freak.

Mirrors don't lie. It's a wonder he could stand to look at you at all.

If I close my eyes, I can still feel the heat burning my skin, hear the screams all around me, feel the sudden impact of the man who tackled me and smothered the flames with his own body.

"I never found out who he was," I say out loud, watching the repulsive way my lips move when I speak, "But he must have d-d-died with the others."

Thirty-eight years old and still talking like a kid caught stealing a candy bar.

I still have nightmares about that day, terrifying dreams where I stand frozen, watching my brother burn, the panicked crowd pressing in around me. Why did I hesitate? If I had acted quicker, I could have gotten to him in time.

I'm sorry I couldn't save you, Sam.

I take out a small jar of burn cream made from my grand-mother's recipe. It's nearly empty, and when it's gone, there won't be any more: The ingredients have become impossible to find, and just like everything else in this godforsaken biodome, when it's empty or spent, we'll learn to do without. I steel myself and then dab on the cold ointment, flinching as it comes in contact with my grotesque flesh. What a cruel joke of nature that skin so ugly can be so sensitive.

I take a slow breath and then continue with my routine, wishing my grandmother was here to comfort me now. When I was a child, she would comb and braid my hair every morning, telling me that I had the hands of a healer and the heart of a lion —and how certain she was that I would be a doctor someday.

You will never be a real doctor, Lani. You traded that for a ticket inside.

I slide my finger across the mutilated flesh on my cheek, haunted by the look of disgust in Miracle Man's eyes when he saw my face. It was as if he could see right through me, see the lies and betrayal and shame.

Lani the fraud. Lani the freak. Lani the whore.

I shut off the light and get dressed in the waning dark, hating my own ugliness, but grateful for the distance my defor-mity affords me, the protection it provides. No man could ever fall in love with someone so hideous. No woman could ever hope otherwise.

Before I leave, I look in on Shannon, sound asleep in her jungle-themed bed. It's still amazing to me that something so beautiful could come from such evil times, but I'm thankful she did. Shannon is the one true and good thing that has come of my life, and I would do anything to protect her.

Still, I dread the day when she hears something about her father and demands the truth.

What will you tell her? What will you tell him?

I tiptoe over to her bed and kiss her on the forehead. "That I love her more than life itself," I whisper.

And nothing else matters.

She opens her eyes. "Bye, Mom. Have a good day. Love you."

"Love you too, baby. See you this afternoon."

I collect my things and start walking toward the radio building, yawning and wishing David hadn't scheduled our meeting at the crack of dawn.

Probably knew I'd be half asleep and that it would make it easier to control things.

Ah yes, David Montelius Kirk, the master manipulator, the man who, twenty years ago, saved me and destroyed me with a single flick of his wrist.

You should be grateful he's still willing to help you.

I glance at my watch and quicken my step.

Yeah, well, he won't be if you're not there when his call comes in.

I've been trying to reach him for weeks, because I need to ask him about the biodome repairs he was supposed to be working on. A section of the wall in sector four collapsed over a month ago, and people are worried, me included. If even a small leak develops, we'll have to evacuate until it can be fixed, and we don't have enough emergency masks for everyone.

I shudder, resisting the urge to go back and make sure Shannon takes hers to school.

She's old enough to make good choices, Lani, and you need to start trusting her.

I force my attention back to the impending radio conference and let out a heavy sigh. At least I won't have to worry about someone staring at my scars. Unfortunately, David's sorry excuse for a wife will probably be there, demanding to know about the guy we found Outside and insisting to her husband that I'm incompetent.

Oka fefe, I hope he keeps that bitch on a short leash.

Problem is, Miracle Man has told me absolutely nothing, and the irony of that is compelling: He's a man who can't remember his past, in a sea of people trying to forget theirs. I know he remembers more than he's letting on, but the guy is an emotional wreck.

"What am I supposed to do, torture him?"

I don't realize I've said it out loud until a D-1 tending the garden in the biodome park gives me a startled look. I smile at him, trying to recall his name but failing. "Figure of speech." I look at him more carefully. "Do you have your mask with you?"

"Yes, Dr. Kai." He pats the pouch on his belt and then goes back to his carrots.

I force myself to jog the last block and manage to get inside, sit down, and put the headset on just as the radio operator points his finger at me.

The instant the connection is made, David's voice booms through. "So tell me about this guy you hauled in from Outside. Where did he come from?"

"He fell out of a tree, David. And good morning to you too."

"A tree? How the hell did he climb up a tree with a biosuit on?"

"He was naked. Not a stitch on him. Didn't you read the report I sent?"

"You expect me to believe that he was Outside without a suit, Lani? Seriously?"

Goddamn, I hate that condescending tone he always uses with me. "Do you think I'm a fucking idiot, David?"

Bella comes on straight away, her voice thin and screechy.

"Don't you speak to my husband in that tone of voice, young lady. And if you knew what was good for you, you'd show a bit more respect to the man who saved your juvenile delinquent ass."

Oka fefe, I hate that bitch. Her so-called husband has spent his whole life sticking his dick into places it doesn't belong, and she still kowtows to him like he's Jesus H. Christ.

"Easy there, girls," David says, his voice amused.

I bite back a retort and continue, "I watched them bring him in through the airlock, folks. He was unconscious and completely naked." I release the button on the mic and resist the urge to kick something.

I can hear Bella's annoyed huff. "I heard there was no serious damage to his head, but if he fell out of a tree, his face must have been pretty beat up. Are you sure no one would recognize him now?"

"Yes, Bella, I'm sure. I know every person in this *okole puka* of a biodome, and he's not from here."

"So where the fuck *did* he come from?" David asks. "He didn't just appear out of thin air at the top of a goddamn pine tree."

I shut my eyes and ask *Pele* for strength. "I don't know. Salt Lake is the closest biodome—over a thousand kilometers and a mountain range away—and they're not m-missing anyone. I checked. The guy doesn't have a single c-callous on his feet, but if you want to contact the other bubs to see if some naked guy went Outside for a stroll and never came back, be my guest."

"Is there anybody other than La-La-Lani we can get to look at this guy?" Bella asks. "If we could send a proper doctor out there, maybe we could find out what's really going on."

"Fuck you too, Bella."

"Now, now, dolls," David says, amusement in his voice.

"That's enough biting and scratching for today. Let me do some more checking on Tarzan and see what I can turn up."

"Be my g-guest." I force myself to continue. "So what about the repair parts you promised for the b-bio—"

"Hey, wait a second," he says, as if he's not even listening. "Remember that guy who claimed to have seen a campfire when he was out scavenging for meds a few years back? Told everyone he found some opened cans of beans and shit?"

"Yes, I remember," Bella says. "I did some research on it. As many as one in five million people may have had some form of genetic immunity to Doomsday. Perhaps we finally found our lottery winner. Did it even occur to you to look into that, Miss Kai?"

"Of course it did," *You idiot.* "I'm analyzing blood samples right now."

"Genetic immunity?" David says. "Maybe we *should* bring him out to C-Bay."

"Uh-huh," Bella says. "As soon as possible. Let someone with the proper training and necessary experience get to the bottom of this."

"Let me know when the taxi shows up," I say. "And, David, darling, maybe you could toss in the blood analyzer repair parts you promised over a month ago?"

Bella ignores my innuendo. "But Miss Kai's report said he was healthy, no signs of malnutrition or disease, not even dirt under his fingernails. Although she clearly didn't put two and two together, it's not the sort of thing you would expect from someone living Outside for the last twenty years—"

"*Oka fefe,* Bella, it seemed obvious. He must have come from somewhere, and if he hasn't been living Outside, there must be a hidden facility somewhere close to the Bub."

"Deep Springs," David says. "There were always rumors."

"If he's from some secret mutant colony," Bella says, "why on earth would he be up a tree without any clothing on?"

"Christ, Bella." David's voice is laden with contempt. "Maybe he was just enjoying the view. I told you I'd look into it, so give it a rest."

There's an awkward moment of silence, and I feel a twinge of sympathy for his wife.

"Lani," he says, "you work on jogging Tarzan's memory. Slip him some truth serum or something."

"Truth serum?" I exhale in disbelief. "Really, David?"

"Whatever," he says. "I expect to have a full report next week. Over and—"

"W-wait!" I say, my hand gripping the microphone so tightly it's cramping. "W-what about the structural problem w-we're having? You told me w-weeks ago you'd l-look into it."

Oka fefe, Lani, stop giving her ammunition to ridicule you.

I close my eyes and force down the voices in my head. "If the w-west end of the bubble sags any more, it could p-pull the whole d-dome down with it. And we don't have enough emergency masks for everyone."

"Don't get your panties in a wad, doc. I'll figure something out."

Bella huffs. "She's not a real doctor, David. Stop calling her—"

There's a click on the connection, and David comes back a few seconds later. "That biodome of yours may be finicky, Lani, but she was my first, and she's tough as an ox. I built her from the ground up with my own two hands, so there's no need to worry your pretty little head."

"David—"

"Tell Madders I'll have something for him next week. In the meantime, find out who that Tarzan guy is, and what he was doing in that damn tree. Over and out."

Chapter 8

Diego: Range of Emotion

"Today, we're going to work on range of motion," Lani says as she washes her hands. "You're well enough to begin working those atrophied muscles, and it's high time you started doing so."

"That sounds like fun."

She helps me off with my shirt. "Torturing you may become one of my favorite pastimes."

I roll over on my stomach. "And I thought you were just doing it to be nice. You know, my best friend in middle school always said that back rubs lead to sex."

"Right." She places her hands on my shoulders.

"Sorry," I say, my brain finally catching up with my mouth. "I didn't mean to put you on the spot. You've been nothing but professional with me, but sometimes I forget it's your job."

"Uh-huh."

I turn and look at her. "In the future, I'll try not to enjoy it so much."

She pushes my shoulders back down. "You do that." She starts by working the muscles in my arms.

"Mmm, that feels good. Thank you."

"You're welcome." She begins moving her hands across my body—from my fingers, up my arms, and across my shoulders—checking that bone is healing to her exacting standards. When she's satisfied that everything is in order, she starts again at the base of my spine, probing each vertebra in turn.

"So," I say, keeping my eyes shut. "Do you remember an inferno in downtown Denver, back before the Doomsday Plague mutated? One that set a lot of buildings on fire, all in a single night?"

"Yeah, sure," she says, her voice a bit distracted. "I was there with friends. It was weird because the firestorm started all at once, and they never said what caused it. Why do you ask?" She slides her hands down my leg. "Bend your knee as much as you can, please."

I do. It's not very much. "Did you run into anyone that day? Anyone who needed help?"

"Not that I recall." She pushes my ankle farther back, bending my knee so much it makes the weakened muscles feel like they're on fire. "You doing okay?"

I grit my teeth. "Yeah. Happy as a clam."

She applies more pressure, and a white-hot stab of pain surges through my thigh muscle. "Ouch!"

"Sorry." She releases the pressure a bit, but not enough to make the pain go away completely. "I know it hurts, Diego, but getting your range of motion back is critical if you want to walk again."

"Of course. Carry on, doctor. I'll try not to squawk."

She laughs. "Squawk all you want, Miracle Man. I'm just letting you know that with injuries like yours, pain is a necessary part of healing."

"Duly noted."

She rubs the aggrieved muscle for a minute and then switches over to the other leg.

I mentally brace myself.

"No need to gird your loins," she says, sounding amused. "I'll take it a bit easier, okay?"

"Thanks," I say as she bends the other leg. It hurts, but it's more of a burning than a stabbing, and I manage not to squawk.

She releases my ankle. "Good. Roll over."

I lie on my back with nothing but my boxer shorts on, while she checks the range of motion in my hips. It's not particularly warm in the room, but sweat is forming on my forehead as I try not to complain about the pain she's inflicting.

At last, she puts my legs down. "All done with the easy part."

"I can't wait for the hard part."

She moves her hands slowly up the inside of my thigh, massaging the atrophied muscles, and when the tips of her fingers slip inside my shorts, I feel myself stiffen.

Christ.

"What about a government fortress inside a mountain?" I ask, repositioning my hips so the tent isn't quite so obvious. "Did you ever hear anything about that? Maybe somewhere in the Rockies southwest of here?"

"A fortress *inside* a mountain?"

"Yeah," I say. "A hollowed-out mountain."

"So *not* a biodome, but someplace safe from Doomsday?"

"Exactly."

She stares at me, and I get the feeling there's something she's not telling me.

"Sorry, but I don't know anything about it," she says in her doctor voice. "Things were chaotic back then, lots of bad shit coming down. And when people realized that the doomsayers might be right—that the world as we knew it was coming to an end—there was mass panic, everyone rushing to get inside before the virus infected them. By some estimates, more people were killed in the stampedes than were killed by Doomsday."

"Christ, that sounds awful."

"Well, it wasn't a picnic." She softens her words with a slight smile.

"How did you manage to get inside?" I ask, working to keep my tone casual.

She moves her hands up to my chest, poking and prodding. "Your ribs are healing nicely."

"Thanks to you."

She nods. "I wish all my patients were as healthy."

I clear my throat. "So how did you end up in the Bub?"

She takes a deep breath. "I had a connection to the man who designed and built this biodome, and he got me in right before it was sealed." She freezes, not meeting my gaze. "But my brother wasn't so lucky."

"I'm sorry."

Maybe Dave managed to build a biodome after I left. And maybe he went after Isabel and brought her inside—possibly to get at her research?

I cling to that thin thread of hope.

"Everyone had loved ones who didn't make it inside," she says. "I'm no exception, and I don't imagine you are either." She goes back to checking my collarbone, her eyes downcast, and we're both silent for a bit.

"Who was the man who built the biodomes?" I ask, knowing the answer before the words are out of my mouth.

"*Is* the man. David Kirk." She slides her hands across my forehead and temple. "He lives out on the East Coast in C-Bay, the largest and newest biodome. Back before Doomsday struck, he had a contract to build habitats on Mars. But once the threat became known, he switched over to building biodomes here, and his idea spread like wildfire."

"Was he working with Elon Musk?" I ask, unable to keep the surprise out of my voice.

"*Elton* Musk." She narrows her eyes. "How come you don't remember any of this?"

I toy with the idea of telling her everything: where we found the sphere, what was going on inside the Magic Kingdom, how I ended up in that goddamn tree, but the words won't come.

She'll think I'm one fry short of a Happy Meal, and who could blame her?

"Well?"

I exhale and then shake my head. "I just don't."

"I'm pretty sure you remember more than you're letting on, Diego." She glances down at her hands and then meets my gaze. "Don't you." It's not a question.

I nod, unable to tell her the truth, but unable to lie to her any longer. "There's something in my blood, some sort of genetically engineered cell that counteracts the virus. I don't know how it works, but it only protects me. It kills everyone else in a matter of minutes."

"What? Why didn't you say something sooner?" She jumps up and tosses me my T-shirt. "We've wasted weeks of precious time!"

"I would have told you sooner, but I was afraid you wouldn't believe me." It sounds lame, even to me.

"My god, Diego, people are going crazy all over the world trying to figure out how you survived Outside." She starts grabbing vials and equipment out of a cabinet. "Just yesterday, an elderly couple in Texas died after stepping out of an airlock without suits. Some idiot had convinced them that the mutated virus story was just an elaborate government hoax, and you were the living proof!"

"*Mierda.* I didn't know, Lani. I'm sorry. I didn't think the gizmos in my blood would be much use to you. They only work with my DNA— the one other guy they injected died in a matter of minutes."

"S-so you're an expert on genetics?" She stares at me, her right eye twitching. "Well, are you?"

"No, I'm not," I say, struggling to sit up on my own, and for the first time, she doesn't offer to help. "But if someone would have told me what was going on, I would have said something sooner." I lift my casted arms in a show of frustration. "Christ, my network access is limited to forty-year-old *National Geographic* specials and animated movies, and no one tells me anything—except to keep doing my goddamn exercises!"

"So you didn't say anything about the biotech in your blood because I didn't ask? Even though we're stuck inside these stinking fishbowls?"

I look away, feeling like a complete jerk.

She sets a tray down on my bed and pins me with a glare. "No more lying to me, Diego. If there are things you don't want to talk about, then have the courtesy to say so."

"Okay," I say, "but I didn't lie to you about my past. I just didn't tell you everything."

"Understood." Her tone softens. "But you can trust me. If nothing else, the last few weeks should have demonstrated that."

I nod, knowing she's right. "I'm sorry."

"Apology accepted. So is there anything else about your medical history I should know?"

I shake my head. "I've told you everything I can remember."

"Uh-huh." She pulls a chair up next to me and sits down. "Well, it would seem I've been running the wrong tests. Is it okay if I draw more blood?"

"Yes, of course."

She picks up my wrist and then rubs her thumb across the back of my hand. "I don't know how much I'll be able to unscramble with the technology we have here, but maybe I can figure out a way to get a sample to C-Bay." She scoots her chair closer. "But unfortunately, we're going to have to do this the hard way."

"Wh—at?" I say, my voice cracking. I resist the urge to pull my hand out of her grip. "I mean, what's the *hard way?*"

She laughs and taps my cast. "Don't worry, Miracle Man. Little kids have it done all the time—or at least they used to. Instead of using the inside of your elbow, I'm going to use the back of your hand."

"Yikes."

She tears open a packet and rubs alcohol on my skin. "And if you sit still," she says, pulling the cap of the syringe off with her teeth, "I'll get you a lollipop when we're done."

Chapter 9

Shannon: Ghost Busters

I use needle-nose pliers to strip the dry, cracked rubber seal off the edge of the mask and then drop the snaky-looking strand of polymer into the recycle bin. "Ew." Just like my favorite actor Indiana Jones, I hate snakes, but they always seem to find me.

I stare at the black, curly thing and cringe.

Come on, Shaz, it's not even alive. If you plan to be a bush pilot, you can't be acting like a lolo D-2 every time you see something unexpected.

I bend over and fish the thing back out of the large barrel—using the pliers—and set it on the workbench. Then I take out my lab notebook and write "Kirk-Hudson Rebreather Mask Analysis" at the top of a new page and add:

1) Removed strip of disintegrating sealant from inside edge of mask; material: elastic polymer, composition unknown.

Maybe I can get Madders to help me analyze it, see if there's something special in the rubber—just like he always says, "Identify the problem, engineer a fix, and Bob's your uncle." I say the last bit out loud, letting my voice push back the ghosts that lurk in this dark, windowless warehouse.

It's stormy Outside today, and all the weird noises and vibrations are giving me the creeps.

There's nothing to fear except fear itself.

Madders says this space used to be completely filled with barrels, boxes, and huge sacks of food, everything from brown rice to canned peaches, but it's nearly empty now. Mom says I had a peach when I was little, but I don't remember it.

I bet they have some at C-Bay. They have everything there.

These days, we get most of our supplies from scavenger parties sent Outside, so there's not much need for long-term storage anymore. On top of that, everything has to be sent through the irradiation chamber—everything except humans, of course. There's no way to be certain there aren't air pockets inside the boxes and stuff, and that takes a lot of time and effort. Some folks think decontaminating every last bottle, can, and box is a waste of resources, but Mom says you can never be too careful.

Speaking of decontamination, poor Mr. C had a rough time of it after I found him Outside. He had the virus in the air inside his lungs, and people were afraid that if we brought him inside, he'd kill all of us. But Mom came up with this idea to fill the airlock with xenon gas, and Madders rigged up a portable ultra-violet lamp to kill any stray viruses. In less than a minute Mr. C cleared the sensors.

Anyway, Madders keeps replacement items for the biodome in here, along with his airplane parts, and he's been letting me use his workshop for my final project.

But it is kind of spooky being alone in sector four.

Just as I set the pencil down, there's a loud groan from the biodome structure. I can feel the vibrations through my feet, and I let out a startled cry. The noise continues for a few seconds and then subsides. I stand there frozen, listening for the alarm, but it doesn't go off.

Probably just the wind, Shaz. Don't be a scaredy-kitten.

Still, I turn and run my gaze across the biodome wall, looking for a bulge or fissure. I stare at a section that is all twisted and roughly patched, but everything looks fine. Mom claims the repair was just a hasty bit of last-minute construction, but Madders says someone set a bomb off next to the bubble. Someone from Outside. It was right after the Bub was sealed, and the explosion ripped a hole in the dome. Lots of Originals were killed before they managed to get the wall in sector four resealed.

I shut my eyes and hold my breath. In my head I can hear those poor people screaming as they try to escape, the virus turning their flesh and bones into sludge just like in the final scene from *Raiders.*

Ick.

Mom says I watch too many movies, and maybe she's right. But this part of the biodome still gives me the heebie-jeebies.

"Nothing shocks me. I'm a scientist." I recite the line in my best Indiana Jones voice, wishing I had a dog to keep me company just like he did.

Maybe someday?

When I'm almost finished cleaning up, I hear the hinges on the warehouse door groan.

"Hey, Shenanigans!" Madders says, his gravelly voice is full of warmth. "How's the investigation coming along? Did you get the mask problem sorted?" He ambles over to the workbench and picks me up in a bear hug, his gray whiskers tickling my ear. "How's my favorite scientist, engineer, and future bush pilot?"

"Great now that you're back!" I say and give him a quick kiss on the cheek. "How much do you remember about making these masks?" I hold up the cracked rubber snake. "I was hoping you'd have some idea what this was made from?"

"Hmm." He puts on his reading glasses and takes a closer look. "Where'd you get it?"

"From around the inside edge of the mask. I pulled it off to get a look at what was underneath, but now I'm thinking that maybe the polymer seal is the problem."

Madders is one of the oldest people in the bubble, and one of the smartest. Mom says he was probably brought in because he could fix and fly planes, but I think it's because he's a genius.

I played chess against him once—bad idea.

He's also the only Original who treats me like an adult, and if my dad were alive, I think he'd be just like Madders—at least I hope he would be.

"So you think maybe the seal is bad—and not the filter?" he asks, still examining the snake.

"At least on this mask. I've been testing it with vapors from all the chemicals you keep—" His bushy eyebrows rise but he doesn't interrupt me. "—and nothing noxious is getting through. So my first hypothesis is that the seal around the edge failed, letting microscopic amounts of the virus in."

"Shannon, that's brilliant! No one has touched these masks in years—not since we ran out of replacements—and I remember being surprised that the new filters didn't seem to work for very long, and that would explain everything." He rubs his whiskers with one hand, thinking for a minute. "Give me a day to dig up my old notes, okay?"

"Ranger that. Thanks for all your help, Madders."

"My pleasure, Shannon. And nice work identifying the problem. You're a fine scientist."

I smile so wide it makes my face hurt.

We give each other a thumbs-up and say our mantra

together: "Identify the problem, engineer a fix, and Bob's your uncle!"

"Exactly." He gives me a warm smile. "You know this could end up saving a lot of lives if the biodome has to do an emergency evacuation."

We hear the wind Outside gust up, and the whole biodome shudders. A worried look crosses his face—and Madders isn't afraid of anything.

My throat gets tight. "Do you think we might have to leave?"

"No, no, of course not." He gives my shoulder a squeeze. "But like your mother says, it never hurts to be prepared. If it's okay with you, I want to tell the Kirks about your discovery."

I nod, proud that he thinks it's important enough to let Mr. Kirk know.

"But," he adds, "I think you should call it quits for today. Your mother mentioned something about math homework."

I try not to frown. "Okay. But I'll see you tomorrow?"

"Looking forward to it already," he says, helping me hang the last few tools on their proper pegs. "Any news on Mr. Miracle?" he asks. "I'm afraid I haven't had a chance to stop by and introduce myself."

"Mom thinks there might be microscopic machines in his body, and that's what kept him alive Outside. Dr. Kirk wants Mom to send blood samples to C-Bay..." I stop and stare at him. "Hey, if you get to take the samples out, can I come with you? Give me a chance to fly in a real single-engine fixed-wing?"

"Not much chance of your mother approving that," he says, "but we can always ask. Now off you go. And don't tell her about using all those flammable chemicals, okay? She'll have me hung, drawn and quartered if she finds out I let you near them."

I jog across the empty warehouse and then open the heavy door. "Of course I won't. I'm not a bimbo, Madders. Toodles!"

It's getting dark Outside as I hurry across the park. Mom's going to be mad that I'm late, but I don't care. Nothing she can say is going to ruin my good mood.

I break into a run, leaping over bushes and setting all the D-2 swings in motion. I know what's wrong with the KRMs, and when I figure out how to fix them, I might just win a Noble Prize.

And then Mom will have *to be proud of me.*

Chapter 10

Lani: The Quick and the Dead

I'm sorting through the newly-arrived boxes of prescription meds, the note lying open on my desk, when Shannon comes bounding through the front door. "Hi Mom. Madders is back!"

I cringe as she slams the door, knowing it can't possibly affect the integrity of the biodome, but still wishing she would be more careful. "Hi, baby. Yes, I know. As you can see, he already stopped by. Please don't slam the door."

"Sorry, Mom." She takes a look at the boxes covering the floor of our small living area. "Wow. They did good, huh?"

"Yes," I say, still thinking about the note. "Better than anyone could have imagined. Have you finished your homework?"

"Not yet," she says. "But I will. Did Madders say where they found all this loot?"

"Mr. Kirk had a hunch about a hospital inside a decommissioned missile silo, and he turned out to be right. Dulce Base was packed with food and medicine, including prescription drugs. Madders ended up flying a centrifuge to Salt Lake and then ferrying medical supplies to Las Vegas and San Francisco."

"So that's what took him so long to get back." She comes over to see what I'm doing. "I have some good news."

I turn the note face down, still uncertain what I'm going to do about its contents. "Oh yeah? How's the final project coming along?"

"Great. Madders thinks I might be right about the polymer leaking. He's going to show me how to make new sealant tomorrow, so I can test it out."

"That's wonderful, baby." I go back to counting bottles, marking each one with a unique number and then recording it in my logbook. I'm on the third or fourth batch of morphine when I realize that I've just written the same serial number on all the bottles.

You're going to have to tell him sooner or later.

"Which means the filters are probably all fine," Shannon says.

"Good to hear." I take the bottles back out and start again.

"And the leprechauns won't need new shoes until next year."

"Uh-huh."

"Mom, you're not even listening to me."

I set everything down, stand up, and put my arms around my most precious possession. "I'm sorry, baby. I'm afraid Madders brought back some bad news about Mr. C, and I'm not sure what to do about it."

"What is it, Mom? Is he going to be okay?"

"Yes, of course." I try to smile. "I'm afraid everyone in his family is dead."

"And he didn't know that already?" she asks, her eyebrows furrowed.

"No. All these years he's been hoping they were still alive."

"Oh." She scrunches up her nose. "And you're afraid that if he finds out they're dead, he might not want to get better?"

I exhale, knowing exactly how he's going to feel. "Yes."

"But you have to tell him, Mom. Anything else would be dishonest."

"I know, baby. But I might wait until he's stronger. Think what a terrible blow it would be to find out everyone you love is dead." I tuck an escaped lock of hair behind her ear. "He'll feel like he has nothing to live for."

"Oh, Mom, you're always expecting things to *go pudding*. Mr. C has you and me to take care of him. We'll make sure he has plenty of love!" She gives me another hug. "You should just tell him. You know you won't be able to sleep until you do."

I nod, knowing she's right about the not sleeping part. "I'll think about it. You get started on your homework, and I'll be back in a bit."

"Sure thing, Mom. Is it okay if I go over to Mindy's after I finish? Mrs. Miller said I could stay over."

"Yes." I grab the note and my sweater. "But finish your homework first."

"Gotcha. Good luck with Mr. C." She moves a box off the couch, plops down, and hauls a heavy book out of her backpack. "You know, Mom, maybe you should marry him."

"Shannon!"

"I know you fancy him. And Lucy says you'd be good for each other. Even if you're too old to make babies, you could still fall in love."

I stare at her, too stunned to speak.

"So maybe it's not so terrible that his family is dead," she says, "because now he has us."

"Shannon Malia Kai. I can't believe those words just came out of your mouth!"

"It's the truth, Mom, and you know it."

"Homework, young lady. Now." She nods, and I walk out

the front door, pulling it hard into the old frame. *"Oka fefe,* what am I going to do with her?"

And what am I going to do with him?

∞

The main lobby of the clinic looks like Christmas morning.

Boxes marked with *CLINIC* are stacked everywhere, and half the people in the biodome seem to be here. Lucy is directing the sorting of everything from baby diapers to bottles of Pepto-Bismol, as everyone munches on an industrial-sized bag of what I can only imagine are very stale potato chips. Diego is sitting in a wheelchair with a small can of grape juice in one hand and a clipboard in the other, his splint-covered legs propped up on boxes.

"Doc!" he says when he sees me. "It's a party! Glad you could join us."

Someone pushes in behind me carrying another box, and I scuttle out of the way. "How did all this get here?" I say to no one in particular.

Lucy hands me a grape juice. "Madders managed to get three semis up and running in Albuquerque. Seems they found the trucks inside an airplane hangar, and Becky says they were all in pristine condition—one of 'em already loaded up with sealed drums of diesel. All three trucks made it back this evening, and they ain't even finished unloading the first one."

"Wow." I set the unopened juice down on the desk.

"But don't worry, doc," Lucy adds. "Every bottle, bag, and box has been going through quarantine, just like you specified."

"Take it easy on the potato chips," I call out. "The oil is probably rancid!"

I notice a box labeled *Kentucky's Finest* and take a quick peek inside. It's a case of bourbon with one bottle already missing. The last time we had that much hard liquor, it turned folks into a mob of self-righteous idiots. I wonder how many more boxes of bad judgment are being unloaded from those trucks?

"Okay, everybody," I say, "we're calling it a night. After nearly two decades in storage, this stuff can wait till tomorrow to be sorted."

Lucy looks relieved. "You heard the doc," she says and starts shooing people out. "Off you go. Thanks for the help."

"Becky?" I ask when it's back down to just the three of us.

"I sent her home to get some rest. She said the interstate was still drivable, but there was the occasional bathtub-sized pothole, so they had to take it pretty slow. She'd been driving one of those trucks for the last twenty-four hours, and I reckon she deserved it."

Lucy takes the clipboard from Diego, and we walk back toward the desk. "What's up, doc? You look like a long-tailed cat in a room full of rocking chairs," she says, keeping her voice low.

"Bad news from Salt Lake." I motion with my head toward Diego. "No survivors."

"Damn. Not what the man needs right now. You gonna tell him tonight?"

I shrug, wishing it wasn't up to me to decide.

"Want me to stay?"

I shake my head. "I'll sleep in the empty room, keep an eye on things until Becky comes in."

"Hey," Diego says, struggling to get his legs off the boxes. "What are you two whispering about? From the look on your faces, someone just died."

I cringe just as he glances up.

"Christ, I didn't mean that literally." He rubs the back of his neck with his good hand, not looking at us, and I realize why he's having so much trouble with his legs: He's cradling a bottle of whiskey between his thighs.

"So what happened?" he finally asks. "Please tell me no one died."

"Not unless you manage to drown yourself in that bourbon," Lucy says and hurries over to help him. "Doc, will you give me a hand getting him settled for the night?"

The two of us manage to get him to the bathroom and then into bed without incident.

"G'night, Mr. C," Lucy says as she fluffs his pillow and then places it back beneath his head.

"Thanks, Luce. You're the best."

"You ain't so bad yourself." She pats him on the arm. "You want me to lock up, doc? What with all the medical supplies stacked out there, I mean?"

"No need. Given that we've been cooped up in this fishbowl for going on nineteen years, I suspect if anything's missing, we'll know where to look."

"Yes, ma'am. I'll check in with you first thing in the morning." She gives me a worried glance and then leaves.

I stand there next to Diego, gripping his bottle of bourbon like it's the only thing holding up the blade of a guillotine.

"So what's the bad news you're trying so hard to hide?" he asks. "Lucy said everyone made it back from the foraging party, and that they found some sort of treasure trove of medical devices and prescription drugs."

"Yes, it's very good news, better than I could have hoped for. I'm just sorry they didn't make it back in time to save you some pain and suffering."

"Thanks." He narrows one eye. "Everything okay with Shannon?"

I nod and glance down at my hands.

"Just tell me, Lani."

"I have s-something for you. Madders b-brought it back

from Salt Lake this afternoon." I take the envelope out of my pocket and hold it out to him. "I'm sorry it's not better news."

He stares at my outstretched hand. "She's dead, isn't she?" His voice is devoid of emotion, and I glance at the bottle to see how much whiskey he's had.

Probably not enough.

When I don't answer, he looks up at me, his jaw set. "Isabel is dead."

"Yes," I say, "I'm sorry. She didn't make it to a biodome in time."

He nods, his face a mask. "Read it to me?"

I set the bottle down on his nightstand and then carefully unfold the note. "Diego Nadales," I say, reading back the name he wrote weeks ago.

"Not me," he says, his voice tight. "Her. Tell me what happened to Isabel."

I check the birthday he has listed for himself and then do the math. He should be close to sixty. "If this is you, why don't you look a day over forty?" I ask, holding the paper out like it can't possibly be correct. "Explain to me how that's possible?"

"Bad luck."

"Diego, when I sent this letter off to Salt Lake, I thought these people were your parents. Are you trying to tell me that *you* are sixty-year-old Diego Nadales?"

"Please," he says. "Just read it. I want to know how she died."

I swallow and go back to the note. "Isabel Sanborn," I say. "Married name Kirkland (or possibly Nadales)." She and the man listed here are the same age. "So, she's your wife?"

"My fiancée. Go on, please."

Someone in Salt Lake has written Isabel's death notice in a loose, loopy cursive:

Fifty-one possible matches (plus or minus six months from date of birth). No survivors.

"Not even one?"

I shake my head. "I'm sorry."

He rubs his face with his hand. "And me? How did I die?"

I stare at him for a sec, uncertain what he means—and then I read off the girly handwriting next to his name:

No match (plus or minus one year from date of birth). Status unknown.

I look up at him. "Of course, you didn't die, Diego, because you're right here."

He turns away from me. "But I don't deserve to be."

"You're wrong about that." I tuck the note back into the envelope and set it underneath the bottle of liquor.

"You should have let me die."

"Please don't say that, Diego." I put my hand on his shoulder, but he shakes it off. "I know you don't believe me, but I know exactly what you're feeling." I walk over to the door and switch off the light. "And it will get better, if you give it time."

"You didn't kill the one person you were trying to save."

If only that were true.

As I shut the door, I hear his first sob, and my heart starts breaking all over again.

Chapter 11

Diego: Shuffle the Cards

At the crack of dawn, Lucy comes waltzing into my room singing "Oh, What a Beautiful Mornin'" and wearing some sort of purple Easter hat.

My stomach feels like someone drove over it with a truck, and my head is wishing it were that lucky.

She opens the blinds, scoops up the empty liquor bottle, and starts getting out my exercise equipment. "Doc says you're well enough to increase the weights *and* the reps, and that means we need to get started directly."

I turn away, unable to face her goddamn cheerfulness.

"Let's go!" she says. "Day's a-wastin'."

"I'm not doing anything."

"Lordy, Mr. C, don't you go spoiling my perfect day. I got myself a fancy hat, some fine new sheets, and there'll be apples for dinner tonight!" She smacks me on the backside, and my temper explodes.

"Goddamn it. Can't you people leave me in peace for one fucking day?"

She stands there in shocked silence, her eyes big, and then

she tucks a loose strand of hair into her hat, her hand visibly shaking.

"Shit, Lucy. I'm sorry. It's not you, it's just..." I stare blankly out the window. "I just want to be left alone."

"Nonsense. We'll fix up that headache of yours, and you'll be good as new." She bustles over to the sink, then offers me three aspirin and a glass of water.

Her hands are still shaking, and I feel like a heel as I swallow her gift. "Thank you."

"Now then," she says, "let's get you up and dressed so's we can start exercising all those muscles Mindy keeps twittering about. Lord knows, Becky's got her hands full with that one."

She sets a new razor, shaving crème, and aftershave down on my nightstand and offers me the wheelchair. "After we finish with your strength training, I thought you might like to take a real shower." When I don't respond, she puts her hands on her hips and gives me a disapproving look. "Or I could just wash you up real good with that new scrub brush Becky brought back."

Lani pokes her head in the door, looking like she had a rough night. "If he gives you any trouble, Lucy, wheel him over to Operations. They mentioned that they could use an extra set of eyes looking up serial numbers for all the nuts and bolts they hauled back."

I bite back an inappropriate response and push myself up into a sitting position, too weak to fight the both of them.

"Now then," Lucy says, straightening out her apron. "After you finish with your exercises, I could use your help putting away supplies." She raises her eyebrows. "Unless'n you intend to carry on like a screen door on a submarine."

"Enough," I say, my tone a bit harsh. "I know what you're trying to do, and I appreciate the thought, but I've had enough. I'd be grateful if you'd just leave me alone."

"Well, bless your heart," Lucy says as she lugs me into the wheelchair. "Everybody in here carrying some heartache, Mr. C, but that don't mean you can just quit livin'. There's still plenty of good to do here and now—plenty of people deserving of your time and affection. And wallowing in the mud ain't gonna help no one, least of all those that care about you."

I glance up at her, feeling like a self-centered jerk.

"I'll pick you up for dinner after I finish teaching," Lani says. "And I signed you up to help the D-1s with homework this evening. Hope that's okay?" She disappears before I can respond, but pokes her head back in a second later. "Love the hat, Lucy. It goes perfectly with that fine embroidery on your apron."

And that's how the next phase of my life begins.

∞

Shannon waves at me and bounds across Central Park, her backpack and blond ponytail bouncing as she lopes across the green space at the center of the biodome. She plops down in the grass in front of my wheelchair and shrugs off her schoolbooks. "Hey, Mr. C. 'Sup?"

Ever since I found out that Isabel was dead, I haven't had a minute to myself. After Lucy administers my grueling morning workout, I shower—which is a luxury around here, and one that I appreciate—and then I help her out around the clinic: folding laundry, washing dishes, and doing other simple tasks. I eat lunch in the cafeteria with the D-2s, and afterwards Becky wheels me out to the park during recess, ostensibly to "get some fresh air."

I spend the afternoons looking through old internet reports on Doomsday and reading what passes for the news now. Lani picks me up for dinner at six, after which I spend the evenings helping the D-1s with math and science homework or teaching folks how to program a computer—Shannon being my best student.

The nights are still long and painful, but I feel like all my wounds are healing.

I set down my book and wave. "Hi, Shannon. How was history class?"

"Same old, same old," she says, slightly out of breath. "I don't know why they make us learn about old white guys. It's not like it matters now. Who cares about a bunch of dead presidents and their failed wars?"

"You got me there," I say. "Any news on your petition to get a dog?"

"No, but Mom says she'll vote in favor. She thinks having a dog in the Bub would be good for us. And Madders says they have a pregnant lassie in the Golden Gate bubble. He promised he'd fly up there to pick up a puppy if the Bub votes yes!"

"You mean a collie."

She wrinkles up her forehead. "Collie?"

"Lassie is a dog's name. Not a dog breed."

"Yeah, sure, Mr. C. Lassie, collie, whatever. She's the only one of her kind, so there's not much sense in calling her a breed, now is there?"

I chuckle. "You're absolutely right."

"They bred her with a Herman Shepherd from the Ashland Bub, and they're calling the puppies *sheplies*."

I don't bother to correct her. "That sounds doggone good."

She laughs. "I'll have to tell Mindy that one." She hops up and moves my wheelchair six inches to the left. "You're s'posed to stay in the Octagon, Mr. C, otherwise you won't get any benefit from the sunlight, and you need calcitriol—you know, vitamin D—for your bones to heal properly." She looks up at one of a dozen transparent areas of quartz on the dome and then down at the circle of light on the grass. When she's satisfied that I'm exactly in the middle, she plops back down in front of me.

"Do you know what happened to your father?" It's something I've been meaning to ask Lani but haven't gotten up the nerve to ask. "Did he not make it inside a bubble?"

"Oh, Mom never talks about him, but I think he died around the same time as her accident. In any case, I don't think she minds being single. She has me and Lucy and the Millers, and with her work at the hospital and the classes she teaches, she doesn't have much time for anyone else." She steals a glance at me. "Except maybe you. And you know she's never been carded..."

"Right."

Her face lights up. "Hey, did you hear that someone in Japan is looking for surviving cats so she can store their DNA and maybe even breed some kittens? Mom says the gene pool isn't large enough to sustain a population, even if there weren't resource issues, but I think she's wrong. Someday we'll figure out how to go back Outside, and then we'll open the vault in the Rockies—and the one in Norway too—and reconstruct a whole world full of lions and tigers and bears."

"Oh my!" I add. "What's in the vaults?"

"They're gene banks, silly. Some buff scientists put them together when things started to *go pudding*. Mom says they have multiple copies of every kind of mammal, and enough human genotypes to repopulate the whole earth."

Isabel's project. Mierda, maybe she did manage to save mankind.

Shannon gives me a worried look. "You okay, Mr. C?"

"Yes, Shannon, I'm fine. Just thinking about all those creatures that landed in the pudding." I take a deep breath and let it out, missing Iz. "Maybe someday you can conjure up a jaguarundi for me?"

"Sure thing." Her face falls a bit. "If I knew what it was…"

"It's a small cat from Costa Rica. You could probably find a picture of it on the net. It's very clever, resourceful, and cute—just like you."

She blushes. "As soon as I find a photo of a jaguarundi, I'll draw you a picture—to remind you of home."

My heart skips a beat. "That would be awesome."

She bites her lip. "I know I should have told you sooner, but I let Jake and Tommy—and Jeremy too—sign my card. Mom says I have to wait until I'm twenty-five to decide on which one first, and by that time you'll be like fifty—so I hope you don't mind that I didn't wait for you."

"Of course not," I say with a smile. "They all seem like nice guys, and I'm sure they're looking forward to practicing with you."

She looks relieved.

"But," I say. "I hope we can still be friends?"

"Of course, silly!" She tosses a handful of grass at me. "And you do know that Mom has the hots for you, right?"

Her assertion makes me uncomfortable, and I shift in my wheelchair.

"It's true, Mr. C. You and Mom make a great couple, and she doesn't mind at all that you can't walk or don't remember anything."

"Good to know," I say to fill the silence. "So, did you decide on your final project? Last I heard, your mother had vetoed your idea to breed rats for pets."

"You mean I haven't told you yet?" Her face lights up. "I'm working on fixing the old KRMs, you know, the Kirk-Hudson rebreather masks!"

"That sounds exciting."

"Yeah, when I first told Mom, she was all 'What a great idea, Shannon!' and 'Won't that be fun to investigate?'" She shrugs. "But she doesn't think I'll actually come up with anything useful."

"Perhaps she was just trying to protect you?"

"From what? Gluing my fingers together?"

I laugh. "You do have a point."

"We have tons of KRMs in storage—more than enough for everyone in the Bub." She sits up straighter. "And I plan to fix them all."

"Wow. If the masks are all broken, how did you rescue me?"

"Using a biosuit, of course." She sits up straighter. "But we only have a few of those, and you have to have special training to use one."

"What if something went wrong in the bubble and everyone had to evacuate?"

"Well, we'd smush people into emergency habitats—but those don't have much food or water, and you can only use them once."

"Yikes. Sounds like you need to fix the rebreathers ASAP."

"Or possibly sooner. Madders—he's the man who *actually* invented the KRMs—told me he once stayed Outside for *three whole months* while sealing the Lou. That's the biodome in St. Louis."

"*Mierda.* Why didn't anyone try to fix them?"

"Everyone just assumed the filters were too old. I remember people who wore masks Outside started dropping like bugs, and as you can imagine, the news spread pretty quick. There were even some places that didn't have biosuits, and they couldn't go Outside anymore."

"Oh, my."

"And besides, masks are really hard to test." She pantomimes breathing through her hands and then choking to death.

"Got it."

"Madders forgot about them until I got the idea to do some testing, and he said there were tons of masks at Dulce Base, so maybe I could fix all of those too, and we could send them to the guys stuck inside."

"Good idea."

"Anyway, Madders was going to talk to the Kirks about it, but I don't want their help. Mom says that Kirk woman didn't do anything with the original mask. She just slapped her name on it so she could look important."

"Sounds like our friend Mr. Kirk found himself the perfect woman."

"He did? She doesn't sound very nice to me."

I shake my head. "I was just kidding, Shannon." Sort of.

She gives me a strange look. "Have you met Mr. Kirk?"

"Nope, never had the pleasure."

"Well, I may get to meet him soon. I've applied for an internship at C-Bay. That's the biodome on the East Coast where they have the biggest university *and* the best hospital."

"How would you get all the way to the East Coast?"

"Duh. In an airplane. Once I'm old enough, I'm going to fly to C-Bay and figure out a way for us to live Outside—people *and* animals. Maybe if you and Mom get married, you could come live there too."

I laugh uncomfortably. "I already promised to marry someone else, Shannon."

She crosses her arms and looks up at me, her jaw set. "But if you didn't get married, then it doesn't count!" She glances up at my face and then flushes. "Oops. That didn't come out right.

Mom says your girlfriend is, um, well you know..." She studies the grass around her feet.

"Yeah, I know."

She takes off her sweater and stuffs it in her backpack. "I'm always putting my toes in my mouth. I try to say the right thing, but the words don't come out right."

"It's okay, Shannon. I know you meant well. Your mother's a wonderful woman, and I'm very glad I met both of you." I swallow. "But I'm not ready for anything serious right now."

"Well Mom said you'd be running like a marathoner—whatever that is—in a month or two, and it would be good for you to find someone else to love."

That one catches me by surprise, and I don't have a ready response.

She doesn't seem to notice. "And she said your boy parts work just fine too."

Lani appears from behind me. "What was it that I supposedly said?"

Shannon jumps up and grabs her backpack. "Hi, Mom. I was just telling Mr. C about the puppies in GG."

Lani looks at me, her eyebrows raised, but doesn't comment.

"Is it okay if I take him back to his room?" Shannon asks in her best cherub voice. "I'll make sure Becky knows he's there."

The doc glances at me and I nod.

"Okay," Lani says. "But don't be late for your afternoon classes. If you're going to be an engineer, you'll need to know calculus."

"I've got it covered, Mom. I'm not a bimbo."

"Shannon Malia Kai!"

"Oops," she says under her breath. "Sorry, Mom. Of course I'll be on time. Thanks for reminding me."

"Apology accepted." Lani glances over her shoulder at me. "I'll be by in an hour to check on you, *Mr. C*."

"Oh, you've no need to worry, *Dr. K.* Shannon has been taking very good care of me." I wink at Shannon, and she grins.

Lani stands with her arms crossed, watching Shannon undo the wheel lock and turn the chair around. As Shannon pushes me back across the park, I hear Lani mumble, "Boy parts, *oka fefe.*"

Chapter 12

Lani: Suit Yourself

I knock on Diego's door and then walk in, forcing down my apprehension. It's high time he got back to living his life.

He looks up from his laptop and smiles at me. "Hey, you. You're early, but I'm not complaining."

I realize that the cuts on his face have finally healed, and he looks even more handsome now—particularly when he smiles.

Enough with the wishful thinking. The last time you let your emotions cloud your judgment, you ended up alone and pregnant.

"I have a surprise," I say and hold up the sports bag I spent the day putting together.

"New legs?"

"Nope," I say. "But something almost as good."

He gives me the eyebrow, and I laugh.

"I had to guess your size, so I hope it fits." I sit down next to him on a small sofa and set the bag on my lap.

"It looks perfect," he says, the corner of his mouth rising, "but to be honest, I've never worn a sports bag before."

"Very funny, Diego."

He closes his laptop, sets it on the small coffee table, and scoots closer to me.

The soft scent of his aftershave reaches me, and I can feel the heat of his body next to mine.

Don't go there, Lani. There's no way he's falling for you—not now, not ever.

I glance over at him, but he's lost in thought, his gaze still on me.

"Everything okay?" I ask.

"Yep, just thinking. Thanks again for getting me the sofa. It's perfect."

"You're welcome. Given that you're stuck here until we get sector four repaired, I thought it might make things a bit more... homey."

"So what's the surprise?"

I rummage around in the bag and then hold up the swimsuit. "*Voilà!*"

He stares at it, looking like I just offered him three-day-old roadkill.

"It's a bathing suit, Diego." I try not to frown. "We're going swimming."

He wrinkles up his nose. "In a swimming pool?"

"No, in the bathtub."

"Hah."

I tap his arm. "The bones are healed, but the muscles have atrophied, so we're going to start in the water."

"Without any casts?"

"It tends to work better that way, Sherlock." I get his wheelchair and bring it over next to the sofa. "Come on, time to try out those new legs."

It takes a minute, but we manage to get him off the sofa and into the wheelchair without incident.

"You're sure… this is a good idea?" He's still breathing hard from the exertion.

"Positive," I say, hoping I'm right. I pick up the swimsuit. "Will you need help getting this on? Once we get the casts off, I mean?"

"No, doctor." He snatches it out of my hand and then holds it up. "Where I come from, this does not qualify as male bathing attire."

"Well, beggars can't be choosers. But if you want to go in your birthday suit, be my guest. I'm sure the rest of the biodome will be thrilled to get a look at your boy parts."

"So how do *you* know about my boy parts?" he asks.

"Physician's privilege."

"Of course. Don't want to tip your hand and appear unprofessional."

"Are you implying that my interest in you is anything but professional?"

"Not at all. You're the most selfless person I've ever met—and also the most secretive." He puts the swimsuit back into the bag. "I'm just saying you should be careful. I may not have disfiguring burn scars to hide behind, but I'm still damaged merchandise."

"Well at least we have that in c-common," I say. "Except—as you so shrewdly pointed out—I look the part."

"Shit." He reaches out to me. "You know I didn't mean it like that."

"So how did you mean it?"

He shakes his head. "It's just that I hate being so dependent on you."

"Because I don't have a medical degree, or because I'm a woman?"

He shuts his eyes, the muscles in his jaw tight. "Lani, I do care about you—and not just because you saved my life." He looks up at me. "And I am attracted to you too, perhaps more than you realize, but I'm not ready to jump back into a relationship."

"Yeah? Who s-says I am?"

Chapter 13

Diego: Over My Head

Except for the two of us, the Rec Center is deserted. Considering how cramped the Bub is since people had to move out of sector four, it's unnerving.

Like it'll be when the biodome fails...

Lani leaves me alone in the men's locker-room, and I spend five uncomfortable minutes impersonating a crippled snake attempting to get back into last year's too-small skin. When it's as good as it's going to get, I wheel myself back into the lobby, hoping the important parts will remain covered.

Lani, who's wearing a man's button-down shirt over her one-piece bathing suit, holds the pool door open and then pushes me through. "I hope you don't mind sandwiches for supper," she says. "I didn't want too many spectators, so I figured now would be a good time."

"Ah. Good idea," I say, still trying to shake off my embarrassment at the pasty white skin and flabby muscles where the casts used to be.

She rolls me backward down a long ramp and straight into the pool.

"Shit!" I lift my arms over my head, trying to keep them dry.

"Don't be a weenie. It's not cold. It's refreshing."

"Refreshing, my ass."

She laughs and steps around in front of me. She's not wearing the shirt anymore, and for the first time, I can see the extent of the burn scars that cover the right side of her body.

Who or what did that to her?

I sit there like a bank teller facing Billy the Kid.

A door opens behind me, and I belatedly lower my arms into the water. A minute later, Lucy joins us in the pool. With Lani walking backward, Lucy pushes the wheelchair forward until the water is up to my armpits, and then Lani lifts me out of the chair.

"Whoa!" I say. "I haven't used my legs in months!"

"Believe it or not," Lani says, "I'm aware of that."

I glare at her, and she stifles a grin.

"Trust me?" she says and gestures with her head. "And Lucy is right behind you."

Lucy steps around, a life jacket under her arm, and gives a parade wave. "Never lost one on my watch," she says and starts putting my arm through the vest.

I shake my head and pull away, not wanting the cold, wet fabric against my skin.

Lucy frowns. "But you could be the first."

"I bet you say that to all your men."

She clicks her tongue and then looks pointedly at Lani. "If we drown him now, we could still get to supper in time for apples."

Lani laughs. "Just set the lifejacket on the deck, please."

"Pride goeth before drowning," Lucy says, tossing the wet heap up on the side.

Lani motions with her head, and my chair disappears.

"Ay yai yai!" I say, flapping my arms and accidentally splashing Lani in the face. "Whoops, sorry!"

The lithe doctor suppresses a smile, easily supporting me in the buoyant water. "Relax, Diego. I've got you." She pins me with her doctor gaze. "But your legs are going to be weaker than you remember, so take it easy. This is not the Olympics."

"Right," I say. "But I'll have you know, I was once an Olympic tap dancer... until I fell in the sink."

I hear Lucy's groan, and Lani steps backward into deeper water. "Try extending your legs. No weight just yet. See if you can touch bottom."

It takes a bit of work, but I manage to get my feet to the bottom. Despite the painful tightness in my legs, the freedom to move is absolutely wonderful.

"Woohoo!" I say. "This is awesome!"

Lani's expression softens, and she slides her palms across my body to my waist, holding on to me. It's been a while since a woman touched me like that, and I feel myself getting hard. "Rest your hands on my shoulders," she says. "I'll be right here if you need me."

Lucy makes a disapproving noise. "My first double drowning."

"Ready to try standing on your own?" Lani asks, and I nod. "Okay, here we go."

She releases me.

My chin bobs in the water for a few seconds, and then my legs pick up the slack. Stabs of pain flit across my calves and thighs, but I ignore them.

"Okay?" Lani asks, her eyebrows raised.

"Yes!" After months of being lifted, dragged, and pushed, it's difficult to put into words just how exhilarating it feels to be supporting my own weight, even if it's in a kiddie pool. I lift my shoulders out of the water, unable to stop grinning.

Mierda, I'm more than a foot taller than she is.

"Easy, Diego," Lani says, putting her hands back on my

waist and looking up at me, her golden eyes full of concern. "Let's take this slowly."

"You have the most beautiful eyes," I say without really thinking about it.

A surprised look flashes across her face, and then there's a sharp pain in my thigh, and the next thing I know, my head is underwater.

A moment later, I feel her hands on me, and I want nothing more than to sweep her up in my arms, whirl her around, and tell her that everything is going to be okay.

We're both going to be okay.

When our heads break the surface, I let out a whoop, kiss her on the mouth, and then wiggle out of her hold and start swimming on my back. After I manage to keep my head above water for a bit, I steal a glance at Lani.

She looks annoyed, even angry.

"It's okay, doctor," I say, squirting water out of my mouth like a whale spouting. "I know how to swim." I paddle in a circle, waving at Lucy.

"Maybe you could have told me that sooner." There's an edge to her voice, but I can't tell if she's mad about the kiss or just miffed that I don't need her anymore.

"Bless my soul," Lucy says, standing in the shallow end with her hands on her hips. "But I'd say you no longer require my assistance."

"Thanks," Lani says. "Go have some apples for me."

"I'll save some for both of you," she says, winking at me as she gets out.

I swim to where the water is shoulder deep and then try standing again. The muscles in my legs have warmed up, and there's almost no pain. I let out a whoop of delight. "This is great! You're a genius."

Lani follows me into the deep end, half smiling at my exuberance.

"Woohoo," I say, "I forgot how good it feels to stand up."

A worried look crosses her face. "It's too deep here, Diego. We should go back to the shallow end."

I put my hands on her waist, still able to touch the bottom. "No worries, doctor. I've got you."

"Please!" She tries to push my hands away. "This isn't helping."

"We'll be fine. Honest. It's your turn to relax."

She glares at me, her brow one thin line.

"Trust me, Lani. If I lose my balance, I'll let go of you and swim back to the shallow end, okay?"

"You're impossible."

"Water, taken in moderation, never hurt anybody." I kiss her on the nose. "And you're beautiful when you're mad. Shit, you have the most gorgeous eyes, golden like a dragon or something."

Her mouth falls open and then she tries to push me away again.

I take a couple of steps to rebalance us. "But if you don't stop doing that, we *will be* going under."

"Damn it, Nadales. What has gotten into you? I'm your doctor not your mistress."

"Ouch."

"Who are you?" She stares at me, her eyes narrowed. "And what really happened to you?"

"I could ask the same of you," I say.

"I have *never* lied to you." Her voice is icy cold.

"Lani, please. I didn't want to lie to you, but I didn't have any other choice."

She goes limp in my arms. "When it comes to lying, there is always a choice."

"If I told you what happened, you wouldn't believe me." I let go of her, and she dog-paddles to the edge of the pool.

"You think I believe you now?"

I watch her get out and then swim toward the shallow end, conflicting emotions ricocheting around inside my chest like popcorn in hot oil.

I enjoy being with Lani, and when she touches me, I'm filled with warmth and light. But it also confuses me, makes me feel strangely uncomfortable, like a part of me isn't here and never will be.

Isabel's gone, mae. She's been dead for twenty goddamn years. It's time to let her go.

And yet the queasiness in my gut remains.

"Stay where you are," Lani says, "and I'll get the chair." She climbs up the ladder, grabs a towel, and tosses it over her shoulder.

I watch her walk the length of the pool, her long black braid swinging back and forth as she pads on the balls of her feet—the movement as graceful and seductive as a geisha. She backs the wheelchair into the water and then turns it around. "I think in a week or two, we'll have you walking again."

I swim into the seat and use my arms to push myself up into a sitting position. "And I'm sure it's going to be a fun-filled fortnight."

"Don't go soft on me now."

"Well, according to your professional assessment, there's nothing to worry about in that department."

She tosses the towel onto my lap. "Let's hope I'm right about the rest of you."

Chapter 14

Lani: Unchained Memory

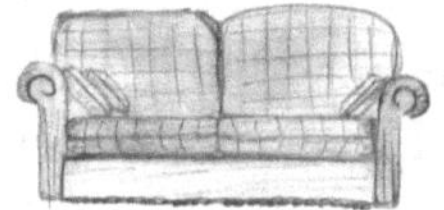

I push Diego's wheelchair toward the Clinic, unable to stop thinking about his "beautiful when you're mad" comment. He's the first man since David to mention the unusual color of my eyes, and the only other man to ever call me beautiful.

The last time David did that was nearly twenty years ago. Doomsday was killing like a Biblical plague in third-world slums and refugee camps, and flights had been suspended. All over the planet, biodomes were being built by the thousands, but anyone with a brain could see that only a tiny fraction of the Earth's population could fit inside.

And then the virus started killing in Mexico City—and shortly thereafter, Los Angeles. Calls went out to institute a lottery, but the rich and famous had no intention of giving up their spots in the lifeboat. Rioting broke out all across the US, and angry mobs attempted to force their way inside the bubbles —why should only the rich survive?

Still, plagues had come and gone before, sometimes killing millions. Humanity survived. Most people just crossed their fingers and got on with their lives. What else could we do?

When two of David's men showed up on my doorstep, I couldn't believe my eyes. My brother peeked out from behind me as they explained that a place in the Kirk Biodome had been reserved for me: "One suitcase, one laptop, no pets." They said I was required to appear the next evening at seven or risk forfeiture, and when I asked about my brother, they glanced down at him and shook their heads. "Only you, miss. I'm sorry."

The Golden Ticket they handed me was worth millions—but I needed two. And I knew who could get me the second one.

"Tell Mr. Kirk I graciously accept," I said. "And that I will save my thanks until I can deliver it personally."

When we arrived the next afternoon, hundreds of people were camped around the biodome. I made arrangements for my brother to wait there with friends, and presented myself at the appointed time, suitcase and computer in hand. I was escorted in through a discreet side entrance where I was scanned, searched, and then made to wait for nearly two hours. There turned out to be a problem with the ventilation system in my sector, so I—and a roomful of other anxious people—were told to come back the following day.

As I was being escorted out, one of David's men caught up with me. He told me that I didn't have to leave, that Mr. Kirk was waiting for me, and would I care to join him? My heart was beating so fast, I could barely answer.

Although David and I had been lovers off and on for months—ever since his StreetSmart team recruited me—I hadn't seen him since he moved into the biodome, and I had missed him. He had always been good to me: getting me into med school, finding the apartment Sam and I rented, paying for my grandmother's funeral. He wasn't married yet, but I knew he had other women—I'd found panties in his car and a lipstick in his jacket pocket—but I clung to the hope that I was different, special. I had never been a girly girl, and with my small chest, narrow hips, and hard-won street smarts, most people treated me like a boy. But David Kirk, the world-famous inventor of the biodomes, saw the princess in me, and I loved him for it.

The first time we had sex was on my seventeenth birthday, and it was the best day of my life. He took me shopping that afternoon and out to an expensive French restaurant that evening. When I didn't like anything on the menu, he handed the waiter a hundred-dollar bill and sent him across the street to buy me a burger and fries. Afterwards, he ordered me two desserts, and while he waited for me to finish, he told me about his boyhood dream to design habitats for Mars and how that dream had transformed into building biodomes here on Earth.

Later, he escorted me to the most exclusive nightclub in Denver. We walked right past the long line outside—the men gazed at him with respect, while the women looked at me with jealousy. The bouncer greeted Mr. Kirk by name, and we were escorted to a reserved table, David shaking hands and slapping backs as we moved through a crowd of Denver's Who's Who. But I told him I didn't like being in the limelight, that I just wanted to be alone with *him*, and we ended up leaving before the drinks even arrived.

He let me drive his Tesla up Lookout Mountain—even though I'd never gotten a driver's license—and I nearly drove it into a hedge. I thought he'd be angry, but he just laughed and showed me how to put it into autopilot. When we got to the top, we walked out on the rocky cliff, the cold wind in our faces, and gazed out at the city lights. He put his coat around my shoulders and held me close while he pointed out the biodome he was building. It glowed like a halo on the horizon.

"I'm going to save them, Lani," he said, the wind tousling his hair.

"Who?" I whispered.

He turned to me, the starlight reflecting in his eyes. "Mankind."

It was then I realized I was falling in love with him.

The guy was amazing—smart, talented, and generous. He saved street kids, built biodomes, gave away millions. He could have any woman he wanted—movie star, athlete, supermodel— and yet, he had picked me. It took my breath away.

I didn't want the evening to end, and after he drove me back to my apartment, I invited him in, insisting that since he'd paid for all my underthings, he should at least get a chance to see them on me.

He had laughed—and then agreed.

It was my first time with a man, and it was incredible— better than I had dreamed it could be.

Even though my days were filled with classes and hospital rounds, I lived for the afternoons David and I spent together. He made me laugh, made me believe in myself, made me dream about the future. I couldn't imagine my life without him. It was the first time in my life I was truly happy.

But as the months passed, I saw less and less of him. And after the Doomsday virus became airborne, I barely saw him at all. I read about his biodomes in the news nearly every day, and I told myself he was too busy saving mankind to squeeze in time for me.

Perhaps I even believed it.

When I arrived at his place that first night in the biodome, I was walking on clouds. I threw my arms around him and kissed him with my whole body. He was happy to see me, but he looked exhausted and his hair had gotten a lot grayer, like the stress of being the most famous man in the world was wearing him down. And I could tell he had been drinking.

He poured us both a Scotch and told me he had missed me —that I was the only person in the world who actually cared about *him*. Everyone else just cared about what he could get them.

He asked me to undress, and I was happy to oblige. I had worn the lingerie he'd bought for me on my birthday, and he recognized it immediately. I knew then that I had won him back.

In the past, he had always been gentle with me in bed, but that night he was rough and vulgar, and it scared me. At one point I went down on him, hoping to please him with something new, and he accused me of fucking other men. When I said no, only him—which was the truth—he slapped me across the face and told me not to lie. I didn't know what to say or do, so I kept quiet and let him do what he wanted.

He had always been very careful not to get me pregnant, so it wasn't until after he came that I realized he hadn't used a condom that night. But what was I going to do, scold the man who had saved my life?

As soon as he came, he got up to use the bathroom. "Bella will be back early, so you need to leave."

"Bella?" I asked like some lolo schoolgirl.

"My soon-to-be wife."

I started getting dressed, my hands shaking so hard I couldn't button my blouse. He watched me struggle for a bit and then stepped closer to help. "It's nothing personal, Lani. I don't love her, but I need her, and it's the only way." It was the first time I'd ever seen him uncomfortable.

I knew it was my last chance to bring my brother inside, so I forced myself to ask him.

He stood there for what seemed like an age, his face unreadable in the dark.

"David, please," I said. "Sam's smarter than I am. He's only eight, but he knows how to program a computer. I'm the only family he has left, and if you don't help him, he'll be alone Outside. Please."

When he found his voice, his whispered response cut like a scalpel. "Is that why you agreed to come here tonight? To suck my dick in exchange for another ticket? Jesus Fucking Christ, Lani, what are you, a whore?" He grabbed my arm so hard it left bruises. "Well, are you?"

"No!"

"Bullshit. You're just like all the other fucking vultures." And then he took his hand back to strike me, but stopped at the last second. "Fuck." He let his hand fall to his side. "Just get out, okay? I'll see what I can do. No promises."

I tried to put my arms around him—to thank him—but he just pushed me away. "Get the fuck out before I change my mind."

It was the last time I was alone with him.

At least you didn't have to suffer the humiliation of him seeing what a deformed monster you've become.

I glance down at Diego in the wheelchair and blink back tears. In eighteen years, the only man who has awakened my shriveled heart finds me physically repulsive.

And who could blame him?

Despite that knowledge, I'm unable to let go of the way he made me feel when he put his arms around me tonight. Safe and expectant and...

Desirable.

Oka fefe, Lani. He's your patient, and you're nothing more than a glorified servant. As soon as he's healed, he'll drop you just like David did.

I know it's true, but my heart refuses to listen.

As I maneuver Diego's wheelchair through the back door of the clinic, Becky rushes down the hall smiling. "It's ready, doc!"

"So soon?" I ask, my heart falling.

"Yessiree," she says. "Lucy had maintenance over there all day fixing it up!" She hands Diego a tray of sandwiches and apples and then gives him a surreptitious wink. "About time you two got a little privacy."

I clear my throat, irritated by the matchmaking that's been going on. "Thank you, Becky."

"You're welcome, doc. Diego's the only one here tonight, so unless you need anything else, I'll be off."

"We'll be fine," I say. "See you tomorrow."

We watch her stride down the hallway and out the front door.

"What's ready?" Diego asks.

"A surprise," I say and start pushing him down the hall. "But it will have to wait until tomorrow. To be honest, I was hoping it would take a few more days to prepare—give you a chance to get stronger—but Lucy and Becky are right: It's high time you got back to living your life."

"Sending me Outside, are you?"

"Actually," I say, "once you're walking, that's not a bad idea. There are hundreds of things that need to be repaired but are nearly impossible to do in a suit."

"Forget I mentioned it."

"But first, I'll have to figure out how to get you in and out without collapsing your lungs. That was a bit dicey the first time around."

"Yikes. I'm glad I was unconscious, but remind me not to make you mad."

I stop and turn his chair around, my hands on my hips. "When have I ever been mad at you, Diego?"

"Are you serious? Twenty minutes ago you were furious with me."

"No I wasn't," I say. "I was frustrated that you don't trust me enough to tell me the truth." I push him back into his room. "I still am."

He cranes his neck around, looking pointedly at the ruined flesh on my face. "Ditto."

"Oh no you don't," I say, positioning his wheelchair next to the sofa. "Not even close. My injury is just a passing curiosity to you. The future of mankind hinges on how you are able to survive Outside."

"Christ, Lani. I already told you everything I know about it, so your argument is total bullshit."

"Good to know." I take the tray of food and set it on the small coffee table. "And although I'm sorry you find me repulsive, my past is none of your business."

"I don't find you repulsive, physically or otherwise, and it annoys the hell out of me that you keep implying that I do." He narrows his eyes. "And I get that you're my doctor. But you keep using that as an excuse to..."

"To what?"

He exhales. "Shit. Never mind."

"An excuse to be professional despite the fact that you wink and joke and kiss me in front of my nurses?"

"I didn't kiss you like we're lovers, Lani."

My breath catches in my throat, but he doesn't notice.

"And it's not me who's winking and casting allusions. But yeah, I haven't done anything to squelch it. I didn't realize you found it so offensive." He looks away. "But I won't make that mistake again."

He sits there with his hands in his lap for almost a minute. "Why don't you take the food and go? I'll get something in the morning."

His dismissal cuts me like falling shards of glass from a smashed mirror.

"You're right," I finally say. "You do make me uncomfortable, but not for the reasons you think."

"So what is it, Lani?" He turns on me, his expression fierce. "What do you say we stop with the doctor-patient bullshit? I haven't told you everything about my past because you wouldn't believe me. But despite what you think, I'm not a serial rapist or a psychopathic killer."

"I never said you were."

"Why am I even arguing with you? You insist on treating me like a child. Nothing I say matters."

"You are the most infuriating, pain-in-the-*akole* patient I've ever met, Diego Nadales. Why do you insist on making it impossible for me to do my job?"

"Can you stop doing your goddamn job for once? Just for ten minutes be real with me?"

"I am being real, Diego. This *is* my life. I'm a mother and a doctor, and the instant I start hoping for more, it'll all come crashing down."

"What are you saying, Lani?"

"I can't go home at night and take off the monster costume, Diego. Not even for you."

"Is *that* what this is all about?" he says, lifting his hands in the air. "Your goddamn scars?" He moves his feet off the footrests and lifts his body with his arms. "I don't even see them anymore, Lani. I haven't for months." He looks over at the couch, calculating how hard it will be to throw himself onto it, and the doctor in me kicks in.

"Don't even think about it," I say. "I didn't spend the better part of a year healing you just to watch you throw it all away because your feelings are hurt."

"I'm not attempting to climb Mount Everest, doctor."

"I d-don't c-care what the f-fuck you're pro-p-posing," I say.

He winces, and for the first time I see a flash of pity in his eyes.

Who couldn't feel sorry for the stammering Quasimodo you've become?

I force down the voices in my head. "Either you let me help, or I'll call Becky back in to s-sedate you, and the two of us will throw your s-sorry *akole* back into bed."

He looks suitably shocked. "You wouldn't."

"If you overstress the muscles in your legs, it'll undo months of progress."

He lets out an annoyed huff, but sits back down in the wheelchair. "And that would look bad on your résumé?"

"Don't fuck with me, Nadales."

He jerks his head around, one eyebrow raised, and then... he smiles, and it disarms me.

I stare at his handsome face, my heart all twisted up in a knot. He's not at all like David—perhaps exactly the opposite—and a part of me can think of nothing except being in his arms again. I want to show him my true feelings—take a chance on finding love.

But you know it would be a mistake. Look how it turned out with David.

He doesn't move, that silly grin stuck on his face.

"What?" I finally ask.

"I think you kinda like me."

"Thank you for cooperating," I say and reach out to him. "And don't worry. I'm a lot stronger than I look."

"I don't doubt that one bit." He places his hands on top of mine, slides his palms up to my wrists, and grabs hold. His touch is cool and strong, and the intimacy of it makes my heart jump into my throat.

Don't go there, Lani. You'll only end up getting hurt.

I pull him up, help him shift ninety degrees, and then lower him onto the couch. "See?" I say. "That wasn't so bad."

He glares at me. "If you use that condescending tone with me again, I'll commit hara-kiri and get blood all over your new sofa."

"I've seen worse." I scoot the tray of food closer to him. "Would you still prefer to eat alone?"

"No," he says. "I'd prefer to have dinner with you—assuming you're not here because of some misguided sense of duty."

"Nope. I'm in love with you."

He exhales. "Right."

"Would you like some tea?" I ask, turning away before he can see my face flush.

"Please."

Oh my god, Lani. What are you thinking? Do you miss crying yourself to sleep every night? You have a daughter and a career. Isn't that enough?

When I'm done making tea, I sit down in the chair across from him and start braiding my hair. "Who are you, Diego? Really."

He watches me, the corner of his mouth twitching, and a wave of self-consciousness washes over me. I adjust my bangs to cover more of my scars.

"I thought you figured that out already," he says and picks up a sandwich.

"Let's see, Diego Nadales, naked tree climber and biotech guinea pig."

"Bingo." He doffs an imaginary hat. "How did you get all those burn scars?"

"Flamethrower," I say and toss the braid over my shoulder. "How did you end up in that tree?"

"Time machine."

I choke on my tea. "Why do you insist on turning everything into a joke?"

"I'm not joking," he says.

"You can't expect me to believe that, Diego."

"Told you so." He gives me a fake smile. "But it's the truth all the same."

"Ignoring the fact that time machines don't exist and that time travel is impossible, you seem to have been totally unprepared to come here. Why would a time machine deposit you at the top of a tree?"

"It was a mistake."

"Pretty fucking big mistake, if you ask me. If Shannon hadn't seen you fall, you'd be dead, Mr. Miracle." I stand up. "I think I'm done listening to this bullshit."

His eyes get big and then his jaw tightens. "Everything I've told you is true, Lani. Everything. But I'm done trying." He repositions his legs in front of the couch and attempts to stand. "So fuck you too."

"Diego, don't!" I rush over just as he collapses against the sharp corner of the coffee table. "Damn it. You are such a stubborn *akole*." I grab him under the arms, trying to wrench him back into the wheelchair, but he jerks away from me.

"I don't need your pity, and right now, I don't want your goddamn help." He throws his arms over the end of the sofa and attempts to pull himself back up. "It *was* a time machine that dumped me in that tree, a time machine from another universe." He collapses onto the cushions, breathing hard.

I reach for him, but his anger scares me, and I pull my hand away.

"I'm from 2025," he says. "And in my timeline, you're still a street kid with a handkerchief and kite string in her pocket to escape the Minotaur."

"What?" The anger drains out of me.

How could he know that?

"The virus hasn't mutated yet, but it will soon. Oh, and there aren't any biodomes. However bad your world fucked things up, it's nothing compared to what's going down in mine."

"Oh my god." I slump down onto the sofa.

"I was part of a top-secret government project to modify the past, stop the Doomsday Plague from happening. The biotech devices in my blood were supposed to help me combat the radiation poisoning I'd pick up diving through black holes, or at least that's what I was told."

"So why are you here?"

He runs his fingers through his hair and pulls one of Shannon's pink rubber bands out of his pocket. "The time machine malfunctioned. Instead of sending me to the past, it sent me to the future." He collects his long, dark locks into a ponytail. "And no one is planning to airlift me out of here anytime soon."

Could he be suffering from a delusional disorder?

"And I didn't tell you this before, because I didn't want to deal with the fall-out—like that 'seriously fucked-up' look you're giving me right now."

Could he be telling the truth?

"It just so happens that my memory is painfully, exhaustively, remorsefully perfect. It may be close to twenty years for you, but everyone I care about died the instant I appeared in your goddamn tree."

"God, I'm so sorry," I say and rest my hand on his leg, unsure what I believe but certain that *he* believes it. "I just assumed that she was... that it all happened..."

"It's okay," he says, his eyes squeezed shut. "It doesn't matter. I know she's dead." He takes my arm, pulls me sideways against his shoulder, and tips his head against mine. "Christ, I don't know what to do with myself."

We sit there, our heads touching and my heart pounding,

until he pulls away to wipe his face. I get up, position the wheel-chair next to him, and reach out.

He shakes his head. "I know you're trying to help, but I don't need a doctor right now."

"How about a friend?" It comes out as a whisper.

He looks up, his eyes wide.

"Come on," I say. "Let's take you home."

He drags his gaze across my scars, and this time, I don't cower or turn away. He meets my eyes. "Will you tell me what happened to you?"

I nod, fighting back tears—and whether they're tears of regret or relief, I couldn't say.

Chapter 15

Diego: Naked Honesty

"Home, sweet home," Lani says as she opens the apartment door. "You're welcome to set up the lock, but most people don't use them."

"That's a key point you have there, doc."

She groans and flips the light switch, but nothing happens. "Oops. We'll have to get someone to look at that tomorrow. And I'll ask them to bring over the sofa from your room too." She enters and turns a light on over the stove. "I know it's small, but it's all yours."

The studio apartment has a tiny kitchenette, a peninsula with two barstools, and what looks to be a Murphy bed all made up in the corner. There's a laundry basket full of my folded clothes on the bed, a stack of canned goods on the counter, and the jaguarundi picture that Shannon drew hanging on the wall.

"It's perfect, Lani. Thank you."

"I thought you needed your own space." She walks into the bathroom and turns on the light. "Electricity seems to be working fine." I hear the toilet flush. "And the plumbing too. Lucy will be in at eight tomorrow to check on you and help with the shower, but if you'd prefer to take one in the evenings, just let me know."

"In the morning is fine."

"Okay." She hesitates. "The mattress is at the same height as your chair, and there are grab bars in the bathroom, so things should be easier for you here. But I'd appreciate it if you didn't overdo it."

"Got it. And sorry about earlier this evening. I'm an ungrateful ass."

"Apology accepted." She walks over to the small window and looks up. "At least for the next week or two, I'd like you to accept help getting in and out of bed." She turns and waits for me to nod. "And as I said, Lucy will be here in the mornings. I'm happy to stop by in the evenings." She looks back out the window. "But if you prefer, I can have Becky come instead."

I smile. "Becky is an excellent nurse, Lani, but I'd prefer to have you."

"Fine." She relaxes a little. "Would you like to take a shower? Rinse off the chlorine?"

Water is a precious resource here in the Bub, and showers are strictly rationed.

"No," I say, "but thanks. It's been a long day, and I'm ready to hit the sack. If you'd give me a minute to use the bathroom, I'll take a hand getting into bed."

The bathroom is just large enough to get my wheelchair in, but I can't turn around or reach the doorknob, so I leave the door open. It's nothing she hasn't already seen or heard before, but it still makes me cringe to appear so inept. Fortunately, the grab bars in the bathroom are well placed, and after I brush my teeth and use the facilities, I back the wheelchair out and position it by the bed.

She's putting canned goods away in the kitchen.

"Ready when you are," I say and take off my shirt, fold it, and set it on the chair by the bed.

She's standing in the kitchen, staring at my chest, and I wonder if she's as uncomfortable with the flabby muscles as I am.

"Lani?"

She doesn't respond.

"Should I put my shirt back on?"

She meets my gaze. "N-no, of course not." I can tell from her voice that she's been crying.

"So what's up?"

"I'm fine," she says, and turns off the light.

I sit there in a shaft of moonlight, wishing I wasn't stuck in a goddamn wheelchair. "Then why are you standing in my kitchen, crying?"

She shakes her head, comes over to me, and pulls down the covers on the bed.

"When was the last time you let someone get close to you, Lani? Other than this evening, when that idiot assaulted you in the pool?"

"Hah." She wipes her face on her sleeve. "Men aren't attracted to... women like me."

"Bullshit. No one even notices your scars anymore. Why won't you tell me the truth?"

She plops down on the bed, her hands and her gaze in her lap. "It's not just the scars, Diego. It's how I got in here, what I did."

"You mean before Doomsday, Lani? That was nearly twenty years ago. What does it matter now?"

She shakes her head, tears streaming down her face.

"Hey." I take her hand and pull her into my lap, and she rests her head against my shoulder. "How old were you, Lani?"

I wait for her to continue.

"Seventeen," she says at last. "I was already pregnant with Shannon, but I didn't know it yet."

"Christ." I put my arms around her. "And the burns?"

"It happened the day they sealed the Bub. Hundreds of people were gathered Outside, desperate to find a way in before the virus got them."

I wait for her to continue, but she doesn't.

"Do me a favor and help me to the bed, please?" I ask, looking down at her.

She jumps up, looking flustered. "Yes, of course."

"Hey. I'm not trying to get rid of you, I'm just tired of sitting in this damn chair."

"Sure." She pulls me up and then lowers me onto the cool sheets. "Would you like me to get your pajamas?"

I shake my head. "But a clean pair of boxers would be great, thanks."

As I attempt to wiggle out of my shorts, she leans over me and slips her fingertips inside my waistband. "Here," she says. "Let me help."

She slides her hands down my body, pushing my damp shorts and swimsuit off. Her touch is light and sensual, and I feel myself getting stiff.

I lie there in the half-darkness, trying to think of a way to avoid the impending awkwardness.

She gets out a clean pair of boxers and then slips them back up my legs. I shut my eyes, hoping she'll completely ignore my hard-on, but just as I lift my hips, she lets out a startled gasp, and for one very long moment, she freezes with her hands on my thighs.

"Maybe you should drop the comments about men not being attracted to you?"

She recovers, lifting the thin fabric over my hard-on. "Well," she says, settling the boxers around my hips. "I can't say I've had that happen before."

I glance down at the tent in my shorts. "And I'm afraid it's not the first time."

"It's not?"

"Well of course not, doctor. You've been stroking and rubbing and caressing me for months. If I didn't know better, I'd guess you trained as a courtesan and belatedly decided to be a doctor because the pay was better."

"Don't say that." She turns away.

"Whoa there, darlin'. I was just kidding. And anyway, I meant it as a compliment."

She doesn't respond, her shoulders rising and falling in the darkness.

"I love the way you touch me, Lani. That's all I was saying."

She turns to me, tears streaming down her face. "I was a whore, Diego."

"A what?"

"You know, a prostitute, a hooker. That's how I paid for med school. And how I got pregnant. And how I stayed alive: I fucked my way into the biodome."

I catch one of her tears with my thumb. "Christ, Lani, you were only seventeen. Whoever used you like that was one messed up bastard."

"David gave me my education, my daughter, and my life."

David? Dave Kirkland is Shannon's father? Shit.

Now that I think about it, they have the same slate-blue eyes.

Christ, you're an idiot. It's been staring you in the face all along.

I exhale. "And you were in love with him?"

She nods once and then brings her hands up to her face. "And then he got bored with me and found someone else."

"Does he know about Shannon? Who she is?"

"I never asked."

I pull her over against my chest and put my arms around her. "So what happened the night they sealed the Bub?"

She settles against me, her heart pounding. "When people realized the doors were closing, they started pushing and shoving—and then they started throwing rocks and trying to destroy the biodome." She exhales. "Men armed with tear gas and flamethrowers were sent out to force the crowd back and protect the walls."

"Where were you in all of this?"

"Up on the ridge, near where we found you." She rests her head on my shoulder. "Just the night before, I had... s-secured my brother's place in the Bub, and that morning I had gone out to get him, b-bring him back inside. But someone started shouting that Doomsday was here in Denver, that people were dropping dead in the streets, that it was the end of the world." She takes a ragged breath. "I guess he was right."

I stroke her back, waiting.

"He was only eight," she says, blinking back tears. "And I was certain David's men would let us pass. They had escorted us to and from the apartment for months, and I was certain they would recognize me."

She takes a slow breath. "It was David who'd given us the tickets to get inside—one for each of us—and I was foolish enough to believe he could protect us."

I hold her tighter, guessing what must come next.

"After I found Sam, I pushed back through the mob, working my way toward the huge loading dock and pulling him along behind. But when the doors started closing, people panicked. I started running the other way, racing toward the small side-entrance I had used the night before. But I couldn't keep hold of him in the stampeding crowd, so I stopped and picked him up." She looks at me, fighting back tears. "But I wasn't s-strong enough to c-carry him and fight the crowd, so I p-put him down again and p-pushed him ahead of me through the panicked bodies."

"You must have been terrified," I say, dread making my throat tight.

"When we finally managed to b-break through, I told Sam to r-run as fast as he could toward the door. David was visible in the window, and I saw him signaling to let us through. I told Sam I'd be right b-behind him." She chokes back a sob. "But other people saw us break away and started following, and the troops panicked." She presses her lips together. "Sam took the full force of the wall of flamethrowers."

"Oh god, no." The image is horrific, and I squeeze my eyes shut.

"And by the time I managed to get to him, my brother was dead."

I lie there for a few moments, unable to speak.

"Christ, Lani, I can't even imagine how horrible that must have been." I hold her against my chest. "I'm sorry."

She lets out a soft cry, and then the floodgates open and twenty years'-worth of bottled-up misery pours out. I lie there with my arms around her and wait for the torrent to subside.

Sometime later, I wake up, and it takes me a minute to remember where I am.

Lani is still clinging to me, her head on my shoulder, the covers pulled up around us. I shift my weight, sliding my hands across her shoulders and back—and realize that she's nude.

Mierda.

It's been far too long since I had a woman in my arms, and

the combination of her naked body and my raw need is electric. My cock jumps to attention.

A moment later, she lifts her chin and kisses me on the mouth, her lips soft and wet. I move my hands up to her head, my heart beating in my throat, and then I kiss her back. She moans and grabs onto my hair, pressing her thigh hard against my cock as she opens her mouth to me.

Somewhere in the back of my head, a little alarm goes off, but it is drowned out by the silent roar of our need.

"God, you feel good," I say and kiss her on the neck and then the shoulder, sliding my mouth across her silky skin. Her breath quickens, and I become caught up in the sound of her desire. "You're so beautiful, Lani."

"Make love to me," she says, her voice trembling.

And I do.

Chapter 16

Shannon: Up in Smoke

I force myself to stay in bed for a full hour past lights out, then quietly get up, change into my warmest clothes, and slip the shoebox out from under my bed.

"Hi, Wilson," I whisper as I peek inside. "You ready?" The mouse puts his front feet on the edge of the box and looks up at me, his cute little nose wiggling. I stroke him on the head, take a dried apple slice out of my pocket, and offer it to him. He scrambles back into the box, holding the apple in his paws and munching away. "Sorry I don't have a sweatshirt for you, little guy. I'll try to make it quick, okay?"

I shut the lid and put my sneakers on. For the hundredth time, I consider telling Madders about my plans, but I don't want to get him in trouble, and even though I'd trust him with my life, I think he might tell Mom. I pull two sweatshirts on over my clothes, pick up the red and white box, and tiptoe out into the dark biodome.

Most of the overhead lights are off, but motion detectors trip as I hurry across the park, lighting my way into the future. I stop in the center of the grass, standing still long enough for the lights to turn off. A thick beam of moonlight shines down through the quartz portal in the center of the dome, and I open the box a tad so Wilson can take a peek.

"A dreamer finds his way by moonlight," I say to Wilson, "and his punishment is that he sees the dawn first."

He squeaks his approval.

Okay, so he's not quite a lassie, but I still love his furry little self.

Five minutes later, I key in the code for the warehouse door and then slip into Madders' lab. There aren't any motion detectors in here, since the supplies are kept locked up, so I take Mom's flashlight out of my pocket and turn it on. The small cone of light pushes back the darkness, and I hurry over to the workbench, trying not to think about the people who died in here.

I turn on the workbench light and put my flashlight away. The mask and plastic ball are right where I left them. I set Wilson's box down and get to work. I found the discarded ball in the Recycling Room, which is the Bub's equivalent of the Room of Requirement at Hogwarts. Madders thinks the ball was used to make "cold cream" which he tried to explain to me.

But eating frozen cow's milk doesn't sound very appetizing, even if Madders thinks it's the cat's purr.

Still, it's a rigid, translucent sphere with a lid, and I already checked that it's airtight.

I put the sphere into a vise to keep it from rolling around and tape a small glass thermometer to the inside.

Wilson noses the lid of his box open, and I lift him out and pet him for a minute. "I hope this works, Wilson, for both our sakes."

I stuff his cotton bed into the ball, toss in another slice of apple, and then put the mouse inside, placing the new Hudson-Kai rebreather mask over the opening. "See you on the other side, little guy."

Getting the new mask to mold properly to the ball is harder than I anticipated, but I eventually manage to get the seal to adhere to the plastic just like it would to a human face. I clean everything up, put Madders' tools away, and switch off the light.

Now for the testing.

I turn on my flashlight, pick up Wilson's ball, and take a deep breath. "There's no such thing as ghosts." I walk deeper into the dark warehouse carrying Wilson and repeating those words.

It's been a couple of years since I was in the deep freeze, but it doesn't take long to find the huge, heavy door. I switch on the room light and open the door. Freezing cold air leaks out through the plastic sheets hanging down inside. I check that the inside is in good working order and verify that the matches are still in my pocket.

"We are all systems go for airtight testing, Wilson."

I step inside the freezer and turn on the light. Nothing happens.

"Shit."

Madders says that word sometimes, and I know that Mom doesn't like it, but it seems appropriate now.

"The light bulb must be burned out."

I peek at Wilson, curled up in his nest. "Here goes nothing."

I pull the huge door shut.

Total darkness surrounds me, and for a split second I can't breathe. I fumble for the flashlight in my pocket, switch it on, and use it to look around the small cave, feeling freaked out.

Just a bunch of cold peas and dead fish, Shaz. Focus.

I sit down on a plastic tub of yeast and set Wilson's ball on a bag of frozen corn, pressing it down a bit so it won't roll off. I check the Mickey Mouse watch that Mom gave me for my thirteenth birthday, set the flashlight down next to Wilson, and then stuff my hands into my pockets. I plan to sing every movie song I

know, hoping that will be enough—and if not, I can always practice derivative rules from calculus.

I smile to myself.

Mom would probably prefer I started with the calc.

I begin with "I'll Make a Man Out of You," the beam of my
flashlight illuminating the shrinking red line on Wilson's thermometer.

After twenty minutes, the flashlight is noticeably dimmer
and my voice is giving out, but the temperature inside the ball
has dropped twenty degrees. Wilson is huddled up inside his
cotton ball bed. "Sorry, mate. But it's for a good cause, and we're
almost done."

I sing "I'm Not that Girl" one more time for good measure
and blow a thin stream of air into the intake valve of the mask.
Wilson pokes his nose out of the cotton, wiggles it a bit, and
then disappears again.

"Air is definitely getting in. Now let's see about smoke."

I take Wilson out of the freezer, check that the door is shut
all the way, and set his ball down on a box. It rolls around a
little, so I take off one sweatshirt and use it to prop up the
sphere. Then I spend a minute getting the circulation back in
my hands and feet.

According to my calculations, the twenty-degree drop in
temperature inside the ball should cause an equivalent drop in
pressure. If the mask isn't completely sealed, air will be sucked
in around the edges. Wikipedia says that smoke particles are
smaller than a virus, so if no smoke gets in, no Doomsday virus
will either.

I light the matches one by one, quickly blowing them out
and then moving the smoking tip around the edge of the mask,
looking for any wisps to appear inside the ball.

After sixteen matches, I'm reasonably sure the seal is good.

"Nice work, Wilson, you passed the first test!"

∞

Ten minutes later, I'm standing in front of the biodome's main airlock, holding Wilson's ball and wishing that Madders was here to watch.

"Identify the problem, engineer a fix, and Bob's your uncle." I take a deep breath. "You ready, big guy?"

I step inside the internal door and tiptoe across the empty room, the crescent moon in the window catching my eye. I check that Wilson is okay and then set the ball down next to the Outside door. "Good luck, Mr. Wilson. If this works, I'll promote you to Dr. Wilson."

I exit the airlock and then secure the inside door. "Here goes nothing."

I lift the protective cover over the controls, enter the keycode, and push the "Start Cycle" button—just like I do when I check on the fish in the reservoir.

The computer display changes to *Waiting for inner portal lock...* then *Verifying containment seal...* and finally, *Opening outer portal...*

I watch the huge door slide sideways past Wilson, swirls of frost forming as the warm inside air meets the freezing winter Outside. Wilson is racing around inside his ball, and I reach for the "Abort" button, sure that the Outside air is killing him. But I know it's too late either way, and I drop my hand to my side, wishing I could have come up with some way to test the mask without risking a life.

I stand there for twenty minutes, watching Wilson's ball making tracks in the snow coming in from Outside. He seems to be getting the hang of making the ball move and is cruising around the room like a champ. I push the talk button and say, "This is Shannon Kai. Please call Matthew Hudson."

I have to wait forty-two long seconds for Madders' gravelly

voice to come on. "Shenanigans? Are you all right? What's going on?"

"We did it, Madders. We fixed the masks. Just like we thought, it's not the filters that are bad, it's the seal. Wilson and I just proved it."

Chapter 17

Diego: Test Her Wings

"Happy birthday, Shannon!" I step inside and give her a bear hug, letting my cane fall to the floor. "Eighteen is a big year, Miss Kai, and I hope it's your best so far." I kiss her on both cheeks. "Thanks for inviting me to your party."

"Of course, Mr. C. You're part of the family." Shannon turns to her mother. "Isn't he?"

"Yep," Lani says, her eyes glossy.

The implication makes me a little uncomfortable, but I let it go.

"Why don't you both sit down," Lani says, "and I'll bring out the cake."

"Cake?" Shannon's eyes get big and her mouth falls open. "You baked me a cake, Mom? I didn't think you knew how to turn on the oven!"

Lani laughs. "I don't, silly. Diego made it for you. He's been over in the West Kitchen slaving away all afternoon."

She gives me another hug. "You're the best!" She hands me my cane. "Come sit down before Mom starts worrying that you're going to trip and kill yourself."

Lani disappears into the small kitchen and then calls out, "And Madders stopped by while you were in class, Shannon. He was really sorry he couldn't be here, but he had to pick up supplies in San Francisco." She peeks around the doorframe. "But he mentioned something about a puppy."

Shannon lets out a squeal of delight. "Thanks for getting the council to say yes, Mom!"

"You're welcome, baby. He mentioned there was a surprise for you in the freezer at the clinic—something about 'cold cream'—but he said he'd be by on Saturday to deliver your real present."

Shannon claps her hands together, bouncing on her toes. "I can't wait. A real dog! I'm going to call her Millie, after Amelia Earhart."

"That's a tail-wagging-good choice," I say, limping across the living room. It's been a month since the splints came off, and although I'm getting better, I'm not going to be running a marathon any time soon. "But what are you going to call him if he's a boy?"

"Earhart," she says. "Not that he'd mind being called Millie. He's a dog after all."

I laugh and sit down on the sofa.

Shannon bounds across the floor and plops down next to me. "So what's the news, Mr. C?" She bumps her shoulder playfully against mine. "Mom says you have something to tell me."

"I do, but why don't you open your present first?" I take a small gift out of my jacket and offer it to her. "It may not be much, but it comes with a whole universe of possibilities. Happy big eighteen, Shannon."

"Thank you, Mr. C." She hugs my arm, and then carefully undoes the wrapping paper and lifts the top off a small box. "Oh my god, you can't give me this!" She lifts the orange seashell out and holds it up to the light. "It's the only thing you have from your old life."

"I think it's high time I let it go." I glance over Shannon's shoulder and catch Lani's smile before she turns away.

Shannon throws her arms around my neck. "Thank you, Mr. C. I love it. Where did you get it?"

"I found it on a beach in Costa Rica a very long time ago."

"It's beautiful."

"I think so too. Maybe someday you can return it for me—I mean after you figure out how to go back Outside, of course—wiggle your toes in the sand and watch the sun go down?"

"I'd like that a lot," she says, turning the shell over in her hands. "I've never seen a real beach—or even a real sunset. Having both at the same time must be wonderful."

"It is." A soul-crushing sadness fills me, and for a second I can't breathe. I promised Isabel I'd take her to see that sunset the night she said she'd marry me.

I miss you, hun.

Shannon's voice brings me back. "So what's the big news?"

I take a minute to clear my throat. "Your mother has arranged for me to undergo some testing at C-Bay. She thinks they might be able to figure out how the machines in my blood keep me alive Outside."

"You're leaving us?" Her voice is full of accusations.

"But I'll be back in a month or two," I say. "Pinkie promise."

She flops heavily against the couch, still turning the shell over in her hands. "You can't leave us, Mr. C. Me and Mom... we need you."

"Mom and I," Lani calls from the other room. "Subjective case pronoun."

Shannon and I exchange looks.

I lean back and put my arm around her. "You don't *need* me,

Shannon. You got along just fine before I fell out of that damn tree. And like I said, I'll be back."

She looks over at me, her eyes pleading, and whispers, "Mom's in love with you, Mr. C, and if you don't come b—"

"Shh." I put my finger up to her lips. "Don't say that. I'll be back. I promise. Hey, I've already fallen hard for both of you!" I jostle her shoulder until she smiles. "Come on, Shaz. It's your birthday, and anyway, I won't be leaving until next week."

Her eyes light up. "Wait a sec!" She scoots to the edge of the sofa. "I'll come with you. Oh my god, it's perfect. I'll take the mask to C-Bay so Mr. Kirk can see it, and I'll teach people how to fix their masks." She looks over at me, a huge smile spreading across her face. "I'm old enough to leave the Bub, and C-Bay has a real university! Come on, Mr. C. You have to take me!"

Lani peeks around the doorframe. "No." She disappears again.

"Maaaaam." Shannon gives me a pleading look and mouths the word, *Help?*

"Your mother's right, Shannon. It's too dangerous. You'd have to wear a biosuit in the plane, and if something went wrong—"

"Madders does it all the time," she says. "He's flown to C-Bay like a hundred times."

Lani reappears. "Absolutely not. End of conversation." She walks into the room carrying my chocolate cake all lit up with candles. "Happy eighteenth birthday, Shannon!"

Shannon's cherubic face is drawn down into a pout, and I nudge her with my foot. She glances sideways at me, her eyebrows furrowed, and I give her my best *Don't go there!* look.

She recovers almost immediately. "Oh, Mom," she says, clapping her hands together. "It's beautiful. And real candles! Thank you so much!" She glances back at me. "But won't they burn the cake?"

I laugh. "No silly. You make a wish, then you get one breath to blow out all the candles. And if you manage to get every last one, your wish will come true."

Lani gives me a disapproving look.

"That is, most of the time," I add as Lani sets the cake down on the coffee table.

"Hmm," Shannon says, her top lip falling over the bottom one. "I wish that everyone..." She thinks for a second. "Every person and every *animal*... could go Outside again." She takes a deep breath and blows out all the candles.

Lani and I clap and start singing "Happy Birthday"—each of us in a different language—as Shannon smiles and blushes.

"That," Lani says, wiping a tear from her eye, "was a very noble wish, Shannon. I love you, baby."

Shannon gets up and gives her mother a bear hug. "I love you too, Mom—more than anything else in the world."

Lani takes a minute to get her emotions back under control, then she laughs and says, "Let them eat cake!" She turns to me. "Diego, will you do the honors? I'll grab some plates and forks."

The instant her mother disappears, Shannon rounds on me. "You have to help me, Mr. C. She'll listen to you. You can tell her that you'll keep an eye on me, make sure I don't do anything dangerous. You know how she is!" She leans closer, her eyes pleading. "Pleeease?"

"I'll talk to her, Shannon, but no promises."

Lani reappears, a tea tray in hand, and I hastily cut the cake.

"Diego, tell Shannon where you got the chocolate," Lani says, her voice light.

"Now there's a story!" I say and hand out the slices of cake.

"Well?" Shannon asks. "Where did you find it? Chocolate is scarcer than chicken's teeth."

"In the Room of Requirement, of course!"

"No way!" Shannon says, her eyes twinkling.

"Yes way. After you told me about it, I went on a real *scavenger* hunt." I take a sip of tea and continue my story. "I managed to dig up thirteen large cocoa powder tins—I'd say they were buried in the five- to ten-year-old strata—and when I dumped, scraped, and disassembled them, I found enough leftover cocoa for the cake."

"Oh my god, that's ace, Mr. C. Thank you!" She polishes off her piece in a matter of seconds, but when I offer her another slice, she hesitates. "We should save some cake for Madders—and for Miss Lucy and the Millers too. They're all part of our family!"

"Of course we will," Lani says, smiling. "There's plenty, so go ahead and have another slice. I'll cut a big piece for Madders, save an extra one for you, and you can take the rest to Mindy's. I think Mrs. Miller is on call tonight, so you should be able to catch Miss Lucy and her at the clinic."

"Sweet." She starts eating her second piece. "So, uh, about C-Bay..." She gives me a furtive glance. "Mr. C thinks it's a good idea. Don't you, Mr. C?"

Lani chokes on her tea.

"Whoa, there!" I hold up my hands. "I didn't say that, Shannon. I said we'll talk about it."

"But you agree with me! I know you do. You saw what I did with the rebreather mask. You know I'm old enough to go!"

"I want what's best for you, Shannon, and so does your mother." I look at Lani. "Whatever your mom says goes."

Lani gives me a scathing look and then turns to Shannon. "In the first place, it's too dangerous. You'd have to be Outside for *days*. One little accident, and unlike Diego, you'd be dead in a matter of minutes."

"I know that, Mom. I'm not a lolo D-2. I go Outside every week to take care of the fishpond, and I've never had an accident. Even when the rattlesnake bit through my suit, I didn't panic, and nothing bad happened. Madders says I'm more mature than most of the adults he knows."

"In the second place," Lani says, "you have absolutely no actual flying experience, so you'd just be extra work for Madders."

"Mom, I've spent hundreds of hours running the simulator. And the only reason I don't have any real experience is because you refuse to let Madders take me up in his airplane."

"And in the third place, you're just a child. The world is a cold and uncaring place, young lady, and you'd be stuck half a continent away from home with no one to take care of you."

"Mr. C will protect me," she says, glancing at me. "And besides, I'm not a child anymore, Mom. If you'd just give me a chance, you'd see that I can take care of myself."

"I absolutely forbid you to g-go, Shannon!"

I've never heard Lani raise her voice before, and I can tell that she is close to tears—and so is Shannon.

Christ, what a mess.

"And Mr. C agrees with my d-decision," she adds, almost begging. "Don't you?"

I take a long drink of tea and finish eating my cake.

"Well, don't you?" Lani finally says, her eyes pinned on me.

I nod, unable to meet Shannon's gaze. "If your mother says you can't go, Shannon... Well, that's all there is to it."

Chapter 18

Lani: Pickup Lines

After Shannon stomps out, Diego and I stand there staring at each other. It's the first time we've been alone together in a couple of weeks—since I pronounced him strong enough to take care of himself—and I can tell that he's uncomfortable.

Because of this absurd idea about Shannon leaving? Or because he doesn't want to be alone with me?

Ever since that night in his apartment, we've been spending more time together, but as soon as things get physical, he backs off. When I finally got up the nerve to ask about it, he said, *Give me some time*, and left it at that.

Still, not a day goes by that he doesn't find a minute to put his arms around me, whether it's a hug first thing in the morning or an all-too-fleeting embrace after he walks me home at night. And I live for those brief moments in his arms.

But there's no way I'm letting him take Shannon away from me.

And Bella wouldn't let you in C-Bay if her life depended on it.

"You could have backed me up a bit better than that," I say.

Diego shifts his weight and then shuts the door. "It would be good for Shannon to get out and meet new people, Lani, get a formal education, and have an opportunity to widen the gene pool."

I stare at his profile, all the warmth drained out of me.

"And from the sounds of it," he says, "C-Bay would be the perfect place for her to do that." He looks up at me, asking with his eyes why I'm being so unreasonable.

"I can't, Diego. I can't let her go. It's too dangerous. What if something were to happen to her—happen to both of you?"

"Nothing's going to happen to us, Lani." He takes my hand and pulls me into a hug.

"You don't know that!" I squeeze my hands into fists. "You haven't been Outside since you fell out of that damn tree." I look up at him, irritated that he won't let it go. "This world is not like yours, Diego. Too many things can go wrong, and small mistakes can be lethal." I turn away. "At least for those of us who don't have biotechs floating around in our blood to protect us."

"That's why we have Madders. He's the best pilot in North America—you said so yourself." He glances down at my face and then pushes a lock of hair behind my ear. "And Shannon says he's flown the route hundreds of times—"

"More like three or four trips in twenty years."

"—so there's no reason to believe he won't get us there safe and sound."

"He's had some close calls: emergency landings and a cracked propeller."

"But he still managed to get there and back just fine."

I rest my forehead against his chest, my thoughts racing. The voices in my head have been mostly silent since I told Diego about Sam, but now that he's planning to leave—and god forbid, take Shannon with him—they've returned to haunt me.

What will you do if he never comes back?

"Once we get there," he says, "Shannon can start on her engineering degree—and also help with the rebreather masks. It's a once-in-a-lifetime opportunity, Lani, and when she graduates, every biodome in the world will be begging her to go live there."

The thought makes my chest hurt.

He gives my braid a gentle tug. "Maybe it's time you let her spread her wings?"

I bite my lip, fighting back tears—but failing.

He watches a tear roll down my cheek. "Shit, I'm an idiot," he says and pulls me back against his chest, stroking my hair. "Look, I'm sorry, Lani. I shouldn't have said anything. If you think it's too dangerous, then it's too dangerous. Whatever you think is best, I'll support you one hundred percent."

His admission makes me cry again.

Because you know he's right.

"Hey?" he says, waiting for me to look at him. When I don't respond, he tips my chin up. "Shannon can stay here and take courses on the computer. Once we get back from C-Bay, Madders can take her flying for real, and the three of us can help her with her classes. We'll figure out a way to make it work, okay?"

I snuggle against him, unable to speak.

He holds me for another minute. "You okay?" He releases me but keeps his hands on my shoulders.

I nod half-heartedly, my emotions a train wreck.

"Did you want me to talk to her about it?"

I press my lips together and then shake my head. "No, I'll do it."

"Okay." He kisses me on the cheek and reaches for the door. "See you tomorrow morning?"

The prospect of being alone terrifies me, and the words

tumble out before I can stop them. "S-stay with me?" My heart is pounding in my throat. "Please?"

He freezes with his hand on the doorknob. "The store kept trying to sell more furniture, but all she wanted was one nightstand?"

I stare at him, not understanding.

"Get it?" He smiles sheepishly. "Sell more furniture...one night stand."

"I should have killed you when I had the chance."

He laughs and closes the door. "So what did you have in mind? A sword fight? Or maybe a battle-to-the-death game of Scrabble?"

"I was thinking more along the lines of bedroom furniture."

He raises one eyebrow. "The nightstand, is it?"

I nod, my face getting hot.

"And Shannon?"

"Sleepover at Mindy's. They're testing recipes for dog biscuits."

"Ah. Good for her."

I swallow. "I was hoping you'd stay the night, actually. I know you wanted some time to think things over, but maybe we could talk and..." I'm unable to finish the sentence.

"Right." He rubs his hand across his mouth, and I fight down the urge to run away.

You need this man in your life—all of him—and you should do whatever it takes to make that happen.

"Are you sure this is a good idea, Lani? Given that I'm leaving in a few days and won't be back for a while? Shouldn't we wait until—"

"Does that mean you don't want to?"

"No," he says. "It means I'm worried about you."

"I'm a big girl. I'll be fine," I say, knowing it's true. "The question is: What about you?"

"To be honest, I'm not sure I can answer that." He moves his gaze across my hair and face. "I know it's time to move on—long past time to move on—but I can't seem to let go of her." He looks down. "When I'm tired, when I'm alone, when I'm in bed at night, I still see her, think about her, miss her." Dark clouds move across his face. "And it hurts. Sometimes it hurts so much I don't want to go on—"

"Shh. Don't say that."

He opens his mouth and then shuts it again. "I just want the pain to stop, Lani. And sometimes when I'm with you, it does. I know you deserve more than that, but it's all I've got to offer right now."

I stroke the side of his face, blinking back tears, and meet his gaze. "If it means you'll stay tonight, I'll take it."

He smiles self-consciously. "Sorry, that wasn't much of a pickup line, was it?" He turns his head, pressing his lips against my palm. "I guess I'm a little out of practice."

I take his cane, lean it against the wall, and put my arms around him. "Your secret's safe with me."

Chapter 19

Diego: Drowning in Hope

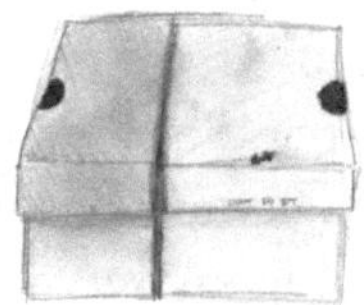

I'm packing what few things I have when there's a knock on the door.

"Come."

I'm expecting Lani to stop by, so I'm caught off guard when a man walks through the door.

"Evening, Diego. Sorry it took me so long to stop by and introduce myself. Been spending more time in the air than on the ground lately." A fit, sixty-something black guy strides across the room and offers me his hand. "Shannon's been telling me all about you, but it's great to finally meet you."

"Matt?" I stare at him, mouth agape.

"At your service." He waits for me to recover and then shakes my hand. "Actually, most people call me Madders. Shannon started calling me that when she was knee-high to a ladybug, as she likes to say, and it sort of stuck."

"*You're* Madders?" Words cannot convey how shocked I am to see him.

"Surprised you, did I?" He pulls up a chair. "Mind if we have a little chat? And I think you might want to sit down too."

"Sure," I say, feeling like I've seen a ghost. "Sorry. I was expecting Lani, and you look a lot like someone I used to know."

He sets a shoebox down on the bed next to me. "So do you." He studies my face. "Only your hair's a lot longer. Which, by the way, looks good on you."

"Uh, thanks. Who's my look-alike with the crew cut?"

"James Nadales. He used to live down the street from me before everything went pear-shaped. I never heard of anyone else named Nadales, even before the shite hit the fan, and when Lani told me about you, I figured you must be related. His son maybe?"

I shake my head. "Who told you my last name was Nadales?"

"Lani, of course. She and I go way back, and she wouldn't have broken your confidence unless she thought it was important."

I shrug. "I guess she knows what she's doing."

"She's convinced your arrival here wasn't an accident, and she thought I should know the truth. But don't worry, I won't spill the beans on how you got here—and Lani hasn't told anyone else, not even Shannon."

"And you believed her?"

He chuckles. "Back before the pandemic, I was a research physicist. My team was looking into wormholes connected to singularities, and I knew people who thought black holes could be used as shortcuts across space-time. Seems they were right."

We sit in silence for a minute, both of us staring at our hands.

"So tell me about James?"

"Be glad to, but I don't remember much," he says. "He disappeared before Doomsday hit. Bad times, those—chaos everywhere. Panicked people were trying to get Inside, and when they couldn't, they tried to take down everyone else with them. It's a wonder any of us survived." He leans forward, his elbows on his thighs. "James is the English equivalent of Diego, isn't it?"

"Yeah, but I've never used it myself. Do you know if James had a wife? Isabel maybe?"

"Nope. Never married as far as I know." He shifts in the chair. "He had a woman living with him when we met, and he managed to get her into the Bub. But she and the kids were killed when some idiot set off a bomb outside the biodome, happened the day after we closed the doors." He shakes off the memory and glances over at me. "But her name was Sophie, not Isabel—real cute and spunky—and her kids were just toddlers."

"Shit."

"Yeah. There was a lot of that flying around back then."

"So what happened to him?"

"Don't know. He wasn't in the biodome when we sealed her up." He shakes his head. "I'm sorry."

"Me too," I say. Sophie was Isabel's roommate when we first met, and I'm left wondering how my parallel self ended up living with her.

Christ, he must have known Isabel too.

"Bloody hell." Matt's mouth falls open.

"What?"

"You're James, right? Only younger?"

I look away, uncertain how to answer—and then decide on the truth. "I'm his parallel from another universe."

"If that's the case, then you should be my age." He looks me over. "And you don't look a day over forty."

"Yeah. I'm twenty years behind you."

He narrows his eyes. "You're not just from another universe, you're from another time?"

"I left my universe right before Doomsday mutated. I was

supposed to travel twenty years into the past, but the time machine's targeting mechanism failed, and I ended up here."

"Crikey. Time *and* space travel." He's quiet for a bit, rubbing his hands together. "That's a lot to swallow."

"It gets better. In my world, *you* built the time machine."

"I did?" He laughs. "Well blow me, no one ever took my research seriously here."

"We were in a place called the Magic Kingdom, a government research facility hidden inside a hollowed-out mountain somewhere in the Rockies. There were a hundred people analyzing two other high-tech gizmos they found inside the Einstein Sphere—along with the time machine plans."

"The Einstein Sphere?"

"Basketball-sized tungsten ball. Weighed a couple thousand pounds. It materialized above Denver going at supersonic speeds, and the resulting impact started a firestorm that took out half of downtown. Never happened in this world?"

"No. What was in the sphere, besides the time machine plans?"

"Instructions for building a quantum-computing device that allowed us to peek into other universes—we called it the Peeping Tom. And designs to create the custom biotech gizmos in my blood."

"Shite," he says. "Seems you're the man of the century."

"More like the failure of the century. I didn't actually *do* anything. My name was inside the Einstein Sphere. That's it."

"So *did* you come here to help us?"

I shake my head. "Like I said, the time machine malfunctioned. The people in my world don't even know your world exists." I exhale. "So what about Isabel? Do you know anything about her?"

"Yeah, I guess you could say that." He points to the box on

the bed. "That's for you. I've been holding on to it for going on twenty years."

I raise an eyebrow.

"Go ahead. Open it."

Inside the shoebox is a folded sheet of paper, a hardwood jewelry box that looks exactly like the one I left on my dresser in the cabin, and an envelope addressed to *Diego Nadales*.

"Christ," I say. "Where did you get this?"

"It appeared in my refrigerator the night the biodome was sealed."

"Was there anything, uh, odd in there with it—like maybe an old sock?"

"Nope," he says. "No dirty laundry. But if the note hadn't warned me about the bomb, everyone in the biodome, including me, would have been killed the following day."

I unfold the note and hold it up to the light. The heavy paper has a Kirkland Enterprises watermark in the middle.

Dave.

The words on the stationery are scrawled in black ink—and it's signed with a stylized capital D.

That bastard. How did he get hold of the time machine? And how did he manage to send something to THIS universe?

I read the note:

HUDSON—

KEEP THIS IN A SAFE PLACE UNTIL NADALES SHOWS UP (AND KEEP YOUR DAMN MOUTH SHUT ABOUT IT!) TOMORROW MORNING, RUN TESTS ON ALL THE CONTA-MINATION SENSORS. DO IT FIRST THING IN THE MORNING.

D—

I set the note down and pick up the wooden box. "So what happened after you found the note?"

"I showed it to David Kirk, but he thought it was a fake: The handwriting looked like his, but the watermark had his company name misspelled."

"Kirkland Enterprises."

"Yeah. Still, I didn't see any harm in following the instructions, so the next morning I spent an hour running the tests. The system was new, and I discovered that the sensors in the new sector hadn't been turned on. I fixed them and was getting ready to leave when the bomb exploded right outside the west end of the biodome—blew the bloody wall to bits. Fifty-seven people died, and if I had been in my apartment, I would have been killed too—and with the sensors offline, the whole biodome could have been exposed to the virus."

"Christ."

He rubs his face. "Just wish I would have thought to hand out masks before I started running the tests..."

"Whoever sent that note to you, didn't *want* you to hand out masks, Matt. He wanted to make sure *you* didn't die, but he couldn't risk changing anything else."

"God Almighty. So who sent it?"

"Dave Kirkland. He's David Kirk's parallel in my universe. How he managed to get all this into your fridge, I have no idea, but I'm betting it involved a time machine." I set the note down and take out the small wooden box. "This was in the refrigerator too?"

He nods. "I hope you don't mind. I opened it to see what was inside." He rubs the back of his neck. "And I read the note too—the envelope wasn't sealed."

"No worries," I say. "Twenty years is a long time to resist opening the cookie jar." I slide my hands across the smooth carved wood, my heart pounding in my throat. "It contains an orange seashell?"

"Bloody hell. How'd you know that?"

"Lucky guess." I open the case and take it out. "I had one just like it in my hand when the time machine dumped me in that pine tree. Shannon found it on the ground next to me and liked it, so I gave it to her for her birthday."

"Why'd you bring it with you?"

"It showed up in the glove box of my car—with a note telling me to take it."

"Damn," he says. "This is making my head hurt."

"Believe me, I know the feeling."

"Any idea what the connection between the shells is?"

"No, but I think they're all identical, possibly down to the atomic level. I bet James had one just like it. And I think this one is from yet another universe."

"Just like you."

I nod. "So why'd you wait so long to tell me about all this?"

He exhales. "When I helped bring you in through the airlock, I thought I recognized you. But you were in no shape for visitors with crazy messages from the past, so I let it go. By the time you were better, I knew Lani had feelings for you, and I wanted to give you a chance to get to know her before I wrecked everything..." He glances down at his hands. "Anyway, I wasn't sure you were the right guy, and after holding on to it for decades, I didn't think a few more weeks would matter." He looks up. "But when Lani told me your last name, and that you claimed you were from another universe, I couldn't rationalize it any longer."

I unfold the note that was in the box with the seashell and read it:

HEY TARZAN—

ISABEL'S ALIVE, BUT IF YOU DON'T GET YOUR SORRY
ASS BACK HERE PRONTO, SHE WON'T BE.
    D—

∞

"Oh my god," I whisper, barely able to breathe. "She's alive."

Lani walks in carrying a stack of my clothes. "Who's alive?" She glances at me, then at Matt, and then repeats her question.

"Isabel," Matt says, not meeting her gaze. "She's alive in Diego's universe."

Lani turns to me, her face ashen, and squeezes her eyes shut.

"Lani—" I say.

She drops the clothes and rushes out.

Chapter 20

Lani: Without a Flight

I stand gazing out into the cloudless sky long after the plane disappears. In the twenty years since Sam died, I have never felt so empty and alone. And now, with Shannon packed and gone, this shabby, backwater biodome feels like a prison.

I press my fingers against my eyelids, trying to stop the tears, but it's no use.

I always knew that someday I would have to let go of Shannon, but I never dreamed it would be like this. And I knew in my heart that Diego was never really mine, but that didn't stop me from falling in love with him.

They say it's better to have loved and lost than never to have loved at all...

But they're wrong.

And now you've lost both of them.

I watch a lone falcon rising with the wind currents, wondering for the millionth time how the birds and reptiles beat Doomsday. I imagine Shannon up there in the sky, looking down on a world that is all new to her, excitement and anticipation spilling across her beautiful face. She is the one thing that has given my life meaning these last twenty years, a solid and powerful reminder of why I deserved to survive. Out of all the lies, deception, and evil that surrounded my failed attempt to save my brother, one good and true thing happened: Shannon.

Go and see the world, Shannon, and when you're done, come home.

If I'm honest with myself, I belong here in this sorry excuse for a biodome. It's my home, and if I were to leave—follow Shannon to another bubble—there wouldn't be anyone here to deliver babies or treat pneumonia. My life is here with Lucy and the others, and I couldn't bear to have something bad happen to them.

Eventually, I turn away and walk back across the bubble toward the Radio Room, my thoughts turning to Sam. Our mother died giving birth to him, and although my grandmother did her best, by the time he came along, she was crippled with arthritis. I was the one who helped him get dressed and tied his shoes and kissed his knee when he fell.

Back in the turbulent days before I met David, I would tuck Sam in at night, stroking his sweet face until his eyelids got heavy, and tell him we were family, *ohana*. And *ohana* means no one gets left behind.

You should have tried harder to save him. You should have figured out a way.

I sit down on a bench in the park, forcing back tears, and try to decide what I'm going to say to David.

Should I tell him the truth—that Diego claims he's from 2025 and came here from a parallel universe via a misbehaving time machine?

Would he even believe me?

I shake my head, uncertain what I believe.

All I know for sure is that Shannon is gone, and Diego is in love with another woman—a woman I thought was dead and buried decades ago.

There's always another woman, Lani—a better woman.

Although I hate myself for even thinking it...

I wish she never existed.

Chapter 21

Diego: Into Thin Air

We fly east, gaining altitude, unbroken grassy plains spreading out as far as the eye can see. I'm the only one in the plane without a biosuit, and this morning was the first time I'd been Outside.

Lani was right: The fact that everyone is wearing biosuits is downright scary. Add to that the knowledge that even the tiniest hole could mean quick and certain death, and I'm beginning to wonder if this was such a great idea.

After a few minutes, I turn and check on Shannon in the back seat. She's fast asleep, her puppy, Bearhart, snuggled up next to her in a special dog carrier. At breakfast this morning, Lani had dark circles under her eyes, and I can't imagine that she and Shannon got much rest last night.

I'm sorry I couldn't be the man you needed, Lani. God knows I tried.

I watch Shannon and her puppy sleep—probably dreaming of each other—and smile when I remember Madders presenting her with that fuzzy bundle of wet tongue and big feet. When Shannon put her arms around the puppy for the first time, the sheer joy on her face had everyone in the biodome in tears, me included. It was love at first sight for both of them, and Earhart quickly became Bearhart.

And the rest, as they say, is history.

I face front, gazing out my foggy window and feeling lost. Shannon is as close as I've ever come to having a daughter, but I realize now that Madders is the one she'll always look up to—the man she loves as a father. Despite the fact that he's worthy of her trust and love, it's tough to know that I'll always be a distant second.

Unlike you, he's been there for her all along.

The thought sets off another round of regrets.

Before stepping into the airlock this morning, I wrapped my arms around Lani, and she clung to me like she'd never see me again.

Perhaps it would be best if she were right.

When the plane levels off, Matt crosses his arms and swivels his chair to face me. "It looks like smooth air all the way to KC, so feel free to fire up all those questions you must have."

I must look troubled because he pats my leg and nods at the dash. "Autopilot. No need to worry. In fact, it's the safest way to fly—if you're lucky enough to have the equipment. If something comes up, the computer will let us know."

"Ah. Okay," I say, although it hadn't even occurred to me.

We spend the next hour talking about the Einstein Sphere, the Magic Kingdom, and the time machine. In this world, many of the same things happened, but in a slightly different order—and a couple of critical things didn't happen at all.

Matt found a reference to a "metal ball" of "unknown origins" in an old newspaper article, but it seems there were no letters sintered on the outside, no $E = mc^2$, and the sphere landed in the woods instead of a city. It did start a small fire, and by the time it had burned itself out, things had gotten so bad that no one bothered to investigate further, and it disappeared years ago.

Matt also dug up some stuff on a quantum computer being developed by Stanford. The scientists claimed they were capturing photons from another universe, but the project went under, quite literally, when the rogue nuke was diverted into the Pacific Ocean and half of California was hit by the resulting tsunami. Things happened just as they did in my world—except that in this universe, Phil and the Peeping Tom team weren't safely inside the Magic Kingdom.

But despite being well behind us in time machines and peeping toms, there was one field where this universe was light years ahead: David Kirk's biodomes.

But why?

That question nags at me night and day. What happened in this universe that changed things? Could it be as simple as the missing Einstein Sphere: Instead of racing to build a time machine, these people built biodomes? Or was there a Magic Kingdom in this world, and their time machine sent James off to yet another universe? My universe?

Christ. If there's a Magic Kingdom here, you need to find it.

If there are any answers to be found, they're locked up inside that hollowed-out mountain. Matt couldn't find anything on the time machine project, but he did find a few references to a top-secret government installation in the mountains. He thinks the place was built during the Cold War, and the description matches what I remember of the Magic Kingdom.

"I'd bet my last socket wrench that underground city exists," Matt says. "And if it does, I'm just the man to find it. Hell, even if no one is inside, think of all the tools and computers they'd have. Crikey, it would be like discovering a buried treasure. Do you have any idea where it is?"

"Unfortunately," I say, "No. I was locked inside for a couple of months, but I don't remember how we got there. The government guys picked me up in the middle of the night—after I'd been awake for nearly twenty-four hours and hiking hard all day. I passed out ten minutes after they grabbed me, so I don't even know for sure how long I was in the car. That mountain could be almost anywhere in Colorado."

"That's what planes are for, mate. There's nothing like a good riddle to keep an old hermit like me occupied. Once I get back to the Bub, I'll start looking for it." He glances back at Shannon who's still asleep in the back seat. "But for right now, we need to get ready to land."

He turns and pats her on the leg. "Hey Shenanigans. Time to wake up."

"Are we there already?" She bobs her head, still half-asleep.

"Yep," I say, turning around so I can see her face.

"We'll be landing in KC in ten minutes," Matt says as he takes the plane off autopilot. "We're going to drop off some mail and take on fuel, but it shouldn't take more than half an hour."

"Ranger that," Shannon says.

"And Roger too," Matt adds, a smile in his voice.

I turn back around and watch the decaying buildings and empty roads slip by beneath us. From this high up, it looks like a vast toy train table with rails and rivers and roads snaking around tree-covered hills and through low-lying towns—only there isn't a child to flip the switch, start the locomotive puffing down the tracks, and bring the scene to life.

And a hundred years from now, it will all be gone.

Matt shifts in his seat. "I don't know how much you know about the Kansas City Refuge of God, but they're not exactly fond of visitors, so they don't get a lot of planes landing. There's no control tower or radio contact, even though they have scads of fuel."

"Okay. But where's the biodome?" I ask.

"There isn't one," Shannon says. "People sealed up the terminal building and an adjoining hotel instead of building a biodome. We learned about it in history."

"They have a generator that keeps up a constant outward air pressure," Matt says. "And so far, it seems to have kept everyone alive."

"But they don't have many people left," Shannon says. "Less than fifty, and if Mom hadn't saved a bunch of them with a whooping cough vaccine three years ago, there might not be any."

Matt nods. "I delivered the vaccine and three hundred pounds of medical supplies, so I don't think we'll have problems, but I usually tell passengers to stay in the plane."

"Makes sense."

"But in your case," he says, glancing over at me. "I'm going to tell them you need to relieve yourself. So if you could hop out and show them your, um, *abilities* before you do your business, it might make them more inclined to fuel me up on the way back."

"Sure," I say. "I could use a chance to stretch my legs."

"Good. And as religious fanatics go, these guys are pretty tame, but you might want to watch your word choice around them, if you know what I mean."

"Right. I'll be on my best behavior."

He glances back at Shannon. "Just sit tight and I'll get us back in the air shortly, okay?"

"Will do," she says.

Matt puts down the landing gear and a minute later, we're on the ground. He follows an old yellow line to the terminal building and shuts down the engine. We watch a handful of suited figures exit the airlock and lumber toward the plane.

Matt gets out, chats a bit stiffly with one of the ground crew, and walks over to the side of the plane to supervise the unloading of some cargo. After a minute or two, he glances up and gives me a discreet nod.

I climb out, forgetting about my headset until it jerks off and slams against the side of the plane. "Shi—oot."

Everyone on the tarmac is staring at me.

I pick up the headphones, set them back on the seat, and then shut the door, trying not to look like an idiot.

There are faces in the terminal windows watching me, but when I meet their gaze, they vanish. Still, I can feel their stares follow me as I walk across the disintegrating concrete looking for a place to take a leak.

This is going to be awkward.

I step behind a broken-down jet bridge, check that there are no obvious eyes on me, and relieve myself.

As I return to the Cessna, I wave to one pair of eyes and catch a quick wave back before they too disappear.

Fifteen minutes later, we're back in the air—tanks full—as the plane ascends into a cloudless cerulean sky.

Chapter 22

Shannon: Yellow Brick Road

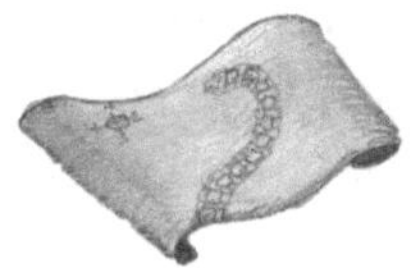

Somewhere around fifty miles outside of St. Louis, we spot the Lou.

"Holy smokes," I say. "It's huge!"

Madders laughs. "If you think this one's big, wait till you see C-Bay."

I lean between the front seats, watching Madders adjust our heading.

He flips on the radio. "St. Louis tower, Cessna one-fower-zero-niner-fife from the Bub. Come in, please." He waits for ten or fifteen seconds and then repeats the hail.

Mr. C gives him a concerned look. "Should I be worried?"

I poke him in the ribs. "It's all right, Mr. C, I'll protect you."

Madders chuckles. "Last time I was here they were having trouble with their equipment, so they were using a hand-held transceiver. If they didn't get it fixed, their signal won't be very strong."

"Which means," I say for Mr. C's benefit, "now that we can see them, they'll be able to hear us. But until we get really close, we're in the drink."

"Hopefully," Mr. C says, "we can keep our heads above water."

"Shouldn't be a problem," Madders says, still smiling. "They knew we were coming, and we're right on schedule."

"Weird how everything is so green," Mr. C says, looking out his window, "but nothing is moving."

"Yeah," I say. "It's hard to believe there used to be so many people." We're flying over what used to be the suburbs of St. Louis. "I've just seen maps and photos, but it looks way bigger in real life."

"How many people are in the Lou?" Mr. C asks.

"About three hundred," Madders says.

"Two hundred and ninety-one to be exact," I say. "The Lou was the second biodome built by Mr. Kirk, and he made tons of improvements over ours. It's four times the area of the Bub, and they have a theater, a bowling alley, and a water park."

"Wow." Mr. C looks suitably impressed. "Sounds like I fell out of the wrong tree."

Madders laughs.

"Mr. Kirk must have been a very busy man."

"Yep," I say. "He personally supervised the building of twenty-three biodomes, and he gave away his patents so that other people could build hundreds more without paying him."

"Hell, that must make him the savior of the world," Mr. C says, not sounding like he means it at all.

"Not many folks alive today who would disagree," Madders says and repeats the hail on the radio.

There's some static and then a female voice comes through. "Matt, are you there? This is Shelly at the Lou, over."

"Shelly, darling, are we ever glad to hear your voice. What's up? Over."

"Matt, there's been an accident. The seal on the east wall failed, and the extra stress on the generator caused it to fail too.

We have everything locked down, but there's no power. Omaha is sending out help, and we have enough O_2 to last until they get here, but there's no way to refuel your plane."

"Bloody hell," Madders says. "Anything we can do to help?"

"Not unless you're carrying a 250-kilowatt generator in your pocket."

"Sorry, Shell, I'm fresh out." He glances at the fuel gauge. "Unfortunately, we're past PNR for KC. What do you advise?"

"Your best bet is to head to Catersville—and hope to hell they don't shoot first and ask questions later."

"Did you say Catersville?" Madders' voice is full of disbelief.

"Yep. According to our records, they have ample fuel reserves." There's a click and a few seconds of silence, and then she comes back on. "Sorry, but I gotta go. Good luck to you. Shelly out."

"Shit," Madders says and cuts back on our airspeed. "Seems we're in for a little extra excitement today, folks."

"What's PNR?" Mr. C asks.

"Point of no return," I say, "when more than half your fuel is spent, so you can't turn around and go back."

Mr. C looks a little green around the gills. "So what's the bad news?"

Madders pulls a chart and a compass out of the door pocket and hands them to me. "Can you take a look, Shannon? Get me a distance and heading for Catersville, please?"

"You betcha!" I unfold the map on top of Bearhart's crate, happy to finally use my navigation skills. My furry ball of puppy love gets up, turns around a couple of times, and then goes right back to sleep.

"Shouldn't we land and see if we can help them?" Mr. C asks.

Sometimes he says the dumbest stuff. "Well," I say, "unless

you have an inflatable biodome hidden in your backpack, there's not much we could do. Without power, everything will be on battery backup, and that won't last long. They have emergency procedures just like we do in the Bub, and we'd just be in the way."

Madders taps his finger against the fuel gauge. "And if we land, we'd be stuck—and that would just add three more people to the evacuation list." He glances over at Mr. C. "Or, at least, two more."

"Right."

"Okay," I say, double-checking my numbers. "Catersville is a bit over three hundred kilometers. Given the current wind speed, you should set the bearing to one-three-eight, give or take."

"Got it." Madders locks in the new course. "Good work, Shenanigans."

"What about Kansas City?" Mr. C says, looking out his window at the huge expanse of lifeless buildings and overgrown freeways. "Maybe we should go back there?"

"Well, we could try, but we'd have to fly around the storm behind us, and as the crow flies, it's a hundred-fifty kilometers farther than Catersville."

"Okay. So what's the next closest choice—besides Catersville?" he asks.

"Omaha," I say. "More than twice as far *and* in the wrong direction."

Madders takes us down a bit, probably to save fuel. "And Omaha is low on petrol reserves. If they fill up our plane, that gives them one less emergency flight out in the future."

The tops of the trees are all covered with blackbirds. Everywhere you look, there are hundreds of them. It reminds me of that scary movie where all the birds go psycho and attack people.

Ick. Better than snakes, though.

"So," Mr. C asks. "What's wrong with Catersville? And what did that woman mean by 'shoot first'?"

"The biodome was built by private donors in record time," I say. "And they sealed it up as soon as it was finished—before there was any real threat. Mom says they only let crazy, old rich guys in, people who believed God was punishing mankind. And Becky told me they force people who break their laws to go Outside without a biosuit."

"I've heard that too," Madders says. "But I think it's exaggerated. In any case, before we land, I want you to cover up with the blanket in back. Keep a low *outline*," he says with a smile. "Once we're back in the air, you and Diego can trade seats, and I'll let you take the controls for a bit, assuming Mr. C doesn't mind."

"Not a bit," he says. "But why have Shannon hide?"

Madders gives him an adult look, the kind that means: *Let's not talk about this in front of the children.* "Why don't you unplug your suit and do a practice run with the blanket, Shannon? Make sure you can fit completely underneath it?"

"Okay, but what about Bearhart?" I ask. "Should I cover him too?"

"No need. Your mother said the sedative would last until we were well inside the Lou, so he should be fine. The little guy will probably just sleep through the whole thing."

"That sounds doggone good," I say and make a show of unplugging my suit.

The instant I get the blanket over my head, I carefully plug my headphones back in.

"...ville is one of a handful of strict fundamentalist bubbles," Madders says, "and they don't take kindly to non-believers—or strangers, for that matter—unless you happen to be young and female. Total wackjobs. They used to do an occasional hostage exchange—you know, expel non-believers and take in new blood —but that hasn't happened in a while. Maybe like ten or twelve years."

"Yikes."

"And Shannon was correct about the biodome being populated by men. What few women they had, died—executed by their husbands, if you believe the rumors."

"Christ."

"Not so much." He glances at Mr. C. "I hope to hell they have fuel and a pumper truck, or we may be getting religion real fast."

I fluff the blanket to show them I'm still doing something back here.

"So you think it's okay to land at Catersville, I mean with Shannon in back?" Mr. C asks.

"No, but what choice do we have? It's not particularly difficult to put this beauty down on any sort of flat surface, assuming we can get the birds to clear out. Trouble is, we'd have to walk from there to the next bubble, and Shannon and I didn't really pack for a cross-country trek in the Tennessee woods."

I've never heard Madders sound so worried, and it scares me. I glance over at Bearhart asleep in his crate, wishing I could stroke his soft puppy fur and tell him that everything's going to be fine.

"But if it comes to that," Madders says, "I'm counting on you to get Shannon to C-Bay. There's a stash of sterilized rations in the back of the plane, and assuming you can fend for yourself, it should last for six weeks or more."

"What about you?" Mr. C asks.

"We'll have to think up some excuse... I'll wander off, or eat a bullet—there's a rifle in back, by the way, but only a handful of rounds."

"What in Christ's name are you talking about, Matt? Suicide?"

"I'm an old git, and I already spent my dime. The food'll last two, three times longer without me. Give you and Shannon a fighting chance."

"Well forget it. We'll just wait here until the rescue party comes for us."

Madders laughs. "You're in the rescue plane right now, mate. There's no way they'd have the resources to come looking for us any time soon, not with the Lou going down and all. It could take weeks, months even, for them to find us—assuming they'd even know where to start looking."

"Then I'll leave you here and go for help."

"Across eight hundred miles of wilderness? I don't doubt that you could make it, but with a bum leg and nothing but the shirt on your back, it'd take you months. We'd be long gone by the time you got back."

"Then we'll all go together. There's gotta be an old highway we can follow. We'd stay out of the swampy woods, rig up some sort of wagon. Shit, who's to say we couldn't find an old car and get the thing running?"

"After twenty goddamn years of rusting in the rain and—"

"Christ on a bike, Matt. Stop talking stupid. I'm not leaving you or Shannon anywhere, and that's that."

"Well let's just hope it doesn't come to that," Madders says. "But if it does, you'll know how to handle it." Before Mr. C has a chance to protest, Madders reaches back and squeezes my knee.

I blink the tears out of my eyes, then peek out from the blanket and give him a shaky thumbs-up. After I spend another minute repositioning the blanket and snuffling my nose, I pretend to plug my suit back in.

"I'm all set," I say, trying to sound cheerful. "The blanket is plenty big."

"Good girl," Madders says, his voice full of false optimism. "Identify the problem, engineer a fix, and Bob's your uncle!"

I just hope Bob wasn't one of the guys who got shoved out the airlock.

We sit in silence for half an hour, listening to the drone of the engine and watching the ground slip past underneath.

At last I spy a straight strip of road running parallel to us. "Freeway at nine o'clock, Madders. If my calculations are correct, it's the Yellow Brick Road. Should take us right to the biodome."

"I see it!" Madders says, banking the plane to the left. "Excellent navigation work, Shenanigans. Once we get out of this mess, you're going to make one hell of a pilot."

A few minutes later, we're flying over the highway. It's overgrown with plants and dotted with derelict cars and trucks, but it still looks like the Yellow Brick Road to me.

Mr. C takes a sip of water from a metal canteen, and I try not to think about how thirsty I'm getting. I could run the recycler in my suit, but that would take battery power I don't want to waste—at least until I know I'll be able to recharge or fire up the solar panels. "Can we make it to Chesapeake Bay on one tank?" I ask.

Madders glances at the instruments. "If Catersville fills us up, we'll need a tailwind and a little luck, but I think it's doable. And the moment we're within visual range of C-Bay, we'll let them know we're out here." He glances back at me. "That way if we run out of fuel, we'll just find a place to set her down and sit tight until they pick us up."

"And you're the most important man alive," I say to Mr. C. "Mom says that Dr. Kirk will do anything to get you to C-Bay."

Mr. C turns around. "*Doctor* Kirk?"

"There!" Madders says and points through the windshield. "You can see the bubble." He flips a couple of switches. "Catersville Approach Control, Cessna one-fower-zero-niner-fife: Do you read me? Over." Madders waits a minute and repeats the hail. "I'll leave it on. Maybe they'll see the plane and invite us for supper."

"Long as it's not the Last Supper," I say.

"Well," Madders says, "if you believe in God, you might want to get on the horn to him right now. We could use all the help we can get."

"Unidentified aircraft approaching from the northwest," says a male voice with an accent like Forrest Gump's, "you have entered restricted air space. Reverse your course immediately, or we will be forced to take action."

We all look at each other.

"It's clearly not a dinner invitation," Mr. C says.

Madders flips a switch. "Catersville Approach Control, Cessna one-fower-zero-niner-fife, twenty kilometers to the west-north-west, inbound for landing. We are from the Kirk Biodome in Colorado. We are on an urgent humanitarian mission and are low on fuel. Repeat: low on fuel. Request permission to land. Over."

There is no hesitation. "Permission denied. Do not attempt to land. You are not welcome at the True Evangelical Church of God's Sacred Ark. I repeat: Do not attempt to land."

"Catersville, this is an emergency. The biodome in St. Louis suffered catastrophic failure today, and it is currently under-going emergency evacuation. They rerouted us here. We do not have enough fuel to continue. I repeat: We are out of fuel. Over."

"You are violating God's commandment to stay out of the Garden of Eden, so he is punishing you. Who are we to challenge the will of God?"

Madders flips off the radio. "Jesus Christ, we're screwed."

"That's it!" I say. "Tell them Mr. C is Jesus, that he can go Outside without protection."

Madders makes a face, but then he looks over at Mr. C. "He certainly looks the part."

Mr. C starts shaking his head, but Madders ignores him and turns the radio back on.

"Catersville," Madders says, "we are transporting the man who was found naked in the Garden of Eden. We believe God sent him to redeem men and their evil ways. Brother D—" He clears his throat. "Uh, Brother James can live Outside without protection, your honor."

He mutes the radio and glances back at me. "Now what?"

"I don't know," I say. "I didn't get that far."

"Bloody hell." He turns the radio back on. "Catersville, I have been instructed by God to fly Brother James to the Chesapeake Bay Biodome. Righteous men are standing by to decipher God's message of mercy. Brother James, the Chosen One, carries the message in his blood."

I nod—but Mr. C slices his hand across his throat, his eyes wide.

Madders ignores him. "Let no man doubt the Hand of God, for He has granted the Faithful an opportunity to witness His miracle. Those who truly believe will know I speak the truth. Over."

They say something indecipherable, and a different voice comes on. "We need to consult the Giver of the Law."

The radio on the other end clicks off, and we all let out a cheer.

"You," Diego says, glancing at me and then Madders, "make quite the pair. I'm surprised you didn't tell them we've got the Ark of the Covenant in back."

Madders shrugs. "Once Shannon came up with the idea, it

was easy. My grandfather was a Baptist preacher. Guess I'm a bit of a natural."

A few minutes later, we fly over the biodome. One quarter of it is collapsed, a loose piece of insulation flapping over a gaping hole on the side.

"That's not good," Madders says. "I wonder how much useful space they have left?"

The undamaged part of the bubble is covered with a thick, black layer of shiny cloth—which turns out to be birds. Thousands of them take flight in one huge cloud as we pass over.

"Bloody hell, I hope they don't dart into our flightpath. That would definitely put paid to our little jaunt."

He banks the plane away, and we get our first look at the airport. There's only one runway, but it looks to be in good condition. I take paper and pencil out of my bag and start drawing a map of the area, just in case we have to land and walk back here.

"Looks like we have a bit of time to kill," Madders says. "So let's see if we can't find an alternate runway, just in case."

"How is it that so many biodomes happen to be right next to airports?" Mr. C asks, looking out his window for a place to land.

"They planned it that way," I say. "The property around the airport was flat and cheap, and getting access to services—electricity, water, gas and such—was straightforward."

"Yes," Madders says. "Most airports had back-up power generators for emergencies, and we made deals to tap into those reserves." He glances over at Mr. C. "Even if you're not a fan of David Kirk, you have to give him credit. He got a lot done back when every day counted."

"There," I say. "Four o'clock. Looks like a good place to put down."

He banks the plane to the west to get a better look. A raised section of concrete freeway stretches out in either direction. It's surrounded by swamp, but straight and flat.

Madders brings us down to within a few hundred feet of the ground. "We'll give them five more minutes to invite us to tea, and then we'll land there and wait."

"What are all those big black things on the road?" I say. "They look too thin to be cars and too big to be—"

"Crikey. I think they're alligators."

"Holy shit," Mr. C says. "I've never seen any that big before."

"I've never seen any in Tennessee before." Madders flies back around, and we take another look. The freeway is littered with huge reptiles sunning themselves. And they don't flinch, let alone dive for cover, when we fly over.

Mr. C glances over at Madders. "You got a horn on this thing?"

"I think if I get close enough, the propeller will scare them." He checks his watch and then takes out the clipboard in his door pocket and makes a note before he circles around to the west.

Dark, heavy thunderheads are massing on the horizon, and there are ominous-looking clouds to the south too. Any way you spin it, in an hour, we'll be at the center of a huge thunderstorm.

Madders glances out at the worsening weather. "I hope to hell they make up their minds soon."

As if on cue, the radio clicks on. "Cessna, this is tower control, you are clear to land on runway four-five right. I repeat: You have been granted permission to land with the stipulation that Brother James will show us God's miracle. Once you have wheels down, you will have five minutes to prove your claim. Do you agree?"

"What happens if we fail to convince you?" Madders asks. "Over."

"You and your airplane will be destroyed for desecrating the Garden of Eden."

"Jolly good. Give us a minute. Over." Madders switches off the mic. "Just bloody great. I always wanted to be an abomination to a bunch of wackjobs." He looks over at Mr. C. "What do you say, Diego? Feel up to walking on water?"

"It definitely worked at KC," I say, looking up from my drawing. "Those guys couldn't take their eyes off you strolling around the tarmac. So I definitely think we should land—but maybe we could check that they have fuel first?"

They both look back at me. "Yeah," Mr. C says. "Good idea."

"Nice map," Madders says when he sees what I'm doing. "I should have insisted that you fly with me sooner."

"Thanks, Mads. Just making use of the view from up here." I finish drawing in the river and hills to the south while Madders circles back around, noting that the main freeway heading east is mostly above water and starts a kilometer or two directly north of the biodome.

He flips the radio back on. "Catersville, Cessna zero-niner-fife. Do you read me? Over."

"What is your decision, Cessna?"

"If Brother James demonstrates his miracle, will you fill us up with one-hundred low-lead airplane fuel? Over."

"We don't have airplane fuel, Cessna, only unleaded gasoline. The last plane that landed here used that."

Madders shuts his eyes. "How long ago was that?"

"Nine, ten years. But I warn you: We will offer no other assistance, emergency or otherwise. If Brother James can prove his miracle, we will refuel your airplane, and then you must leave. Immediately. Any other action will have dire consequences."

Madders looks at Mr. C, who nods.

"We agree," he says. "Over." He turns the plane around and then starts preparing to land.

The thunderheads are nearly on us.

"Okay, Shannon," Madders says. "Stay down and keep your body covered." He glances back at me. "I'll get us out of here as quickly as possible."

I put my drawing stuff away, unplug my suit, and disappear under the blanket.

Chapter 23

Diego: Walk on Water

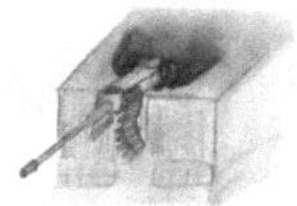

I reach back and pull the blanket over Shannon, wondering for the hundredth time what it would be like to have a child of my own.

Did James and his Isabel ever meet? Did they fall in love like Iz and I did?

The questions bump around in my head like bowling balls, smashing into things and setting off a rush of sorrow and regret that makes my chest hurt.

Did he get her pregnant? Did she tell him? Christ.

I do the math and decide that if they did have the baby, he or she would be a couple of years younger than I am now.

Would I recognize my own child?

There's this part of me that has latched on to the possibility that James and his Isabel made it inside the Magic Kingdom. Maybe her last name was different, just like Dave's, and maybe that's why they aren't in the records. Assuming that they have the sphere, it's possible that his name was inside it too, and that Picasso figured out early on that the writing was hers and brought her in.

It's possible.

They'd be in their sixties now.

Mierda.

Five minutes later, our small plane taxies up to a large, corrugated metal building. Parked in front is a fuel truck behind a wall of jeeps, one of which has a machine gun mounted at the rear.

Matt laughs. "Afraid of automatic coffee pots, but they're goddamn happy to outfit an army with M2s. What a bunch of sanctimonious hypocrites."

There looks to be around ten people in biosuits sitting in the jeeps, but the driver's compartment of the truck is empty. Matt shuts down the engine, and the propeller slows to a stop.

The original voice comes over the radio. "You have three minutes to demonstrate God's miracle."

I take off the headset, glance over at Matt, and open the door of the plane. "Be right back." I stretch my legs for a minute—we've been sitting for the better part of five hours—and then climb down onto the crumbling tarmac. I walk to the front of the plane and then glance up at Matt.

He gives me a goofy thumbs-up.

I walk up to the closest jeep and stand with my hands at my sides, palms out.

There's a lot of wild gesturing inside the jeep two to my left —the one with the machine gun—so I turn and walk over to the driver's side and peek in.

I don't know what I was expecting, but it wasn't a look of abject terror. I lock eyes with the driver, forcing my face into what I hope is a look of universal love and peace, then nod and walk back to the plane.

Matt is laughing when I climb back in, and I ask with my eyes if it's safe to talk.

"Well I'll be a bum-rag if that wasn't the best display of a miracle these folks have ever seen." He glances over at the jeeps.

"Did you see the driver with the M2 in the rear? He'll have to change his pants when he gets back inside."

Large drops of rain smack the windshield.

"You doing okay, Shannon?" I ask.

"Happy as an oyster. Are they going to give us the fuel now?"

"Let's find out." Matt flicks on the radio. "Okay, boys. You saw the miracle. Either give us the fuel or shoot us. If we wait much longer, that storm is going to be on us, and we'll never get out of here alive. Over."

"We hear you, Skylane. We're waiting for the Giver of the Law." Just as he finishes speaking, a vehicle appears around the end of the building: an expensive-looking SUV with tinted windows and a massive antenna sticking out of the top.

Goddamn government vehicle.

I'm half expecting Agent Dick to step out when a raspy female voice says, "He Who Is Most Holy is here to witness God's miracle. Brother James must present himself to The Reverend of Light as God created him. So it has been spoken, so it shall be done." There's a pause. "Now."

I glance at Matt and then start to take off my sweatshirt, but he reaches out to stop me. "Brother James just showed thirteen of God's army that he can go Outside without a biosuit. That was the deal. Why do you insist on denying the miracle?"

The woman's voice is sharp as a knife. "How dare you question the Messenger of God! Your insolence shall be punished by the—"

The tirade stops abruptly and an old man's voice, calm and soothing, comes on. "Easy there, sugar. We don't want you blowing a gasket." He clears his throat. "May those who have witnessed the miracle live to tell their great, great grandchildren, but I have seen the evil and insidious nature of Man, and I know that looks can deceive. If Brother James has been granted the gift of life in the Garden, then let him walk through Eden in the fashion in which God intended. If he fulfills my request, your fuel will be provided."

The woman adds, "So it has been spoken; so—"

Matt switches off the mic. "I'd swear I've heard the man's voice somewhere before, but I can't place it."

I start untying my shoes. "He was President of the United States when I left twenty years ago. Too bad we didn't pack any chocolate donuts."

Matt gives me a curious look.

"Inside joke. Sorry." I climb out of my clothes and pile them at my feet.

"Did you undo your ponytail?" Shannon asks from under the blanket. "It would give you a bit more of the Jesus look, if you know what I mean."

"Right." I pull the rubber band out, letting my hair fall around my shoulders.

"Yeah, that's better," Matt says, placing his hand on my bare arm. "Be careful. Anything funny happens out there, you high-tail it back to the plane. I'll get us out of here quicker than they can say 'Jesus Fucking Christ.'"

I climb awkwardly out of the plane, feeling totally exposed. I no longer use a cane, but I have a pronounced limp —and probably will for the rest of my life. I stand there for a minute in my bare feet, trying to muster as much dignity as a naked man in a world full of biosuits can. The wind has picked up, buffeting my hair and other body parts, and with the sun behind heavy clouds, the temperature is dropping fast.

I shiver as I hobble across the gravel-covered tarmac toward the Grand Imperial Poobah. Lightning flashes in the distance, but it's still too far away to hear any thunder. I stop ten feet from the massive SUV, my hands at my side, and take a deep breath with my mouth open wide enough for them to see that there's nothing inside.

The old man's voice comes out from under the hood of the car. "Raise your arms and turn around."

I do a painful three-sixty, the sharp gravel cutting into my feet, then lower my arms. There are splotches of blood on the tarmac all around me.

"Speak to me of this miracle the Lord has given you."

What?

This is more Shannon and Matt's thing, and I resist the urge to look back at the plane.

The car hood booms again. "Show us that you know the one, true God."

Show us that you're not an asshole who manipulates people for his own gain.

I stand staring at the opaque windshield of the SUV, trying to decide what I can say that won't get all three of us shot.

I'm not much of one for memorizing poems, let alone Bible verses, and I can't think of a single one. I could do the Gettysburg Address in a pinch, but I don't think that's going to cut it here.

Think, Diego.

The only movie I can think of is *Shrek*, but I'm pretty sure it had a song with a couple of Bible references in it—and the word hallelujah. It's the best I can come up with on short notice.

So before I have a chance to chicken out, I shut my eyes and take a deep breath.

"I heard there was a secret chord that David played, and it pleased the Lord..."

And standing there on the disintegrating tarmac in what used to be Catersville, Tennessee, dark storm clouds shifting above my naked body, I attempt to sing a song from a kid's movie.

And although I could use a talking donkey and a chorus of backup singers, I think it does the trick, because when I open my eyes, the jeeps have parted like the Red Sea, and someone is getting into the fuel truck.

I don't know the second verse, so I stand there looking up at the gathering storm, errant raindrops splattering against my face and chest.

"Go with God," says the President. The SUV backs away from me and then disappears behind the terminal building, followed by the jeeps—all except the one toting the M2.

I hobble back to the plane, the gashes in my feet becoming more painful with every step.

When I get close, Matt leans over and pushes open the door. "Now that was something."

I climb back inside and shut the door. "Everything okay in here?"

"Yep," he says. "Nothing to report."

"I'm fine," Shannon whispers. "Madders told me what happened. Cool song, Mr. C."

"Good thing you made me watch that movie," I say. "Could have been ugly otherwise."

Matt waits for me to get dressed. "There's a first-aid kit under your seat. Don't know how much is in it, but help yourself."

I use my sock to brush the asphalt off my bloody feet and then apply pressure.

"You going to be okay?"

"Yeah. It's just a bunch of small cuts. I haven't been barefoot in a while. I guess I should have practiced less on water and more on asphalt."

He chuckles. "I'm going to check on the refueling. I'll be right back." Matt opens his door and hops down on the ground. The armed jeep bursts into action, barreling around the fuel truck toward us. The suited figure in back loses his balance and nearly falls off, and when he recovers, makes a show of aiming the machine gun directly at Matt's chest.

He scrambles back into the cockpit. "Bloody hell. It's my fucking plane, and they expect me to sit here and watch a bunch of twits sabotage it?"

"Everything okay?" Shannon asks, her voice anxious.

"No worries, Shenanigans." He glares at the suited figure driving the jeep, and I'd swear he's resisting the urge to flip him off. "Once we get out of here, we'll put down and make sure everything's sorted."

The fuel truck pulls up to the plane and a minute later, the truck engine gets louder.

Matt continues staring out the window, but his expression relaxes a bit. "Well, at least that's a good sound—means the fuel pump's working."

A guy in a heavily patched biosuit gets out of the truck and begins to unwind a hose.

When he starts pulling it toward the plane, Matt swears and opens the door again—but thinks better of it when the machine gun operator fires a couple of rounds just above the plane. "Goddamn that trigger-happy moron. One spark and we're all dead."

Matt jumps on the radio. "Catersville, the fuel truck driver needs to attach a ground wire to the plane *before* he inserts the hose nozzle, or he's going to blow us all to kingdom come." He waits for a response, but the radio remains silent. "There should be a wire that unreels from the pumper. If you'd let me get out, I can do it myself."

There is more gesturing inside the jeep, and then the driver stops walking and looks over at them. A minute later, he sets the hose down and returns to the truck.

"And can you tell that guy to lay off the machine gun? If it throws a spark in the wrong direction, all that fuel of yours is going to be wasted in one giant fireball, and it'll probably take the biodome with it. Over."

The driver pulls a wire out from a spindle on the truck, but it jams after only a couple of meters. He struggles with it for a minute and then glances over at the jeep driver.

Matt looks like he's going to hit someone. "Let me help him, for Christ's fucking sake."

I cringe, but no one starts shooting.

Another guy gets out of the jeep and then hands his rifle back to the driver. His suit is faded and also heavily patched, and he walks with a bit of a limp. He ambles over to the fuel truck and pulls on the wire with the first guy, but it doesn't budge. They stand there with their helmets touching for a minute and then walk back over to the jeep. The two of them haul a metal tow chain out of the back and proceed to drag it across the tarmac.

"That just might work," Matt says. "If they ground it properly to the truck and make sure it's touching metal on the plane, it should equalize the static charge."

I look back at the two suited figures hobbling away from us. "What if it doesn't?"

"We won't be around to complain."

We watch the two guys wrestle a ladder out of the truck and position it next to the wing. The rain starts coming down harder, the wind blowing it at a forty-five-degree angle. "Shit. That's all I need, water in the tank."

Matt flips the radio back on. "Can you have them block the rain with—"

The ladder bumps against the wing, rocking the plane, and Shannon's puppy starts barking like someone's trying to cut off his tail. He's inside a sealed crate, but the sound carries.

"Shh," Shannon whispers. "I'm right here."

The puppy settles down.

Matt repeats the request to block the rain, and as soon as he releases the talk button, a voice says, "Who else is in the plane with you?"

Matt doesn't hesitate. "No one. It's just the two of us."

A second later, my door opens and someone pokes a rifle barrel into my ribs. "Get out."

"Hey," I say, lifting up my hands. "Easy there. We didn't—"

He grabs my elbow and drags me out of the plane.

"What the hell do you think—"

The butt of the gun slams into my ribs. "Shut up."

I try to grab the stock, but he knees me hard in the groin, and I land heavily on my side.

"Fucking long-haired wetback ain't no miracle. I told 'em that, but they never listen to me." He kicks me in the gut. "What's the trick, asshole? You got some sort of secret cure you ain't sharing with us?"

I try to roll up onto my hands and knees, but he shoves me down hard onto the tarmac. Someone puts a boot between my shoulder blades, pinning me down.

The first guy reaches into the plane and pulls the blanket off Shannon.

"Well, look-ee what we got here. Nice o' y'all to deliver us such a pretty young thing."

Chapter 24

Shannon: The Supreme Sacrifice

I hear frightened voices—and then someone yanks off the blanket.

I let out a startled yelp.

Bearhart starts barking again, but before I have a chance to calm him down, an old guy in a shabby biosuit grabs my wrist and drags me out of the plane. I jump down on the tarmac, my heart pounding in my throat—and see Mr. C lying face down on the ground, some guy's foot on his back.

"Mr. C! Are you all right?"

I hurry over to help him, but the old man catches up with me and pulls me back. "He's fine, little missy. Mikey there is just teaching him some manners. Ain't ya, Mikey?"

"That be right, Grizzly. Just teachin' him some—"

"No he isn't," I say. "He's hurting him. Let him up!" I turn and look at the guy holding on to me. His face is covered with a tangled nest of gray whiskers. "Please. He's the only human who can survive Outside, and we have to figure out how he does it before all the biodomes fail."

"Lord Almighty," Grizzly says, grinning, "if you ain't a firecracker. What's your name, sweet pea?"

"Shannon," I say, trying not to sound scared. "Who are you, and why are you trying to hurt us?"

"Shoot, if we'd known you were in the plane, missy, we would have rolled out the red carpet."

The guy holding down Mr. C laughs. "Mercy, I ain't had a blond in near on twenty years, and you look ripe for the picking."

Mr. C tries to grab the guy's ankle, but the man kicks him hard in the side. "You want us to shoot you, you keep that up, dirt face." He kicks Mr. C again.

"Stop that!" I say as Mr. C curls up on the gravel, his face all bloody. "What are you, criminals?" It's the worst thing I can think of to call them.

I try to jerk my arm out of the old man's grip but he won't let go. "Now, now, little lady. Don't you go getting yer dander up. Mikey is just protecting hisself." He motions with his gun toward Mr. C, and two more biosuits grab him from behind and lift him up.

"And I kin guarantee you won't have no time to spend worrying about biodome failure with all that baby-making we got planned. Ain't that right, Grizzly?"

Mr. C struggles to get loose, and the old guy raises his rifle.

"Mr. C, no!" I say. "Stop! All of you stop!"

"You heard the lady," Grizzly says, grinning at Mr. C but not lowering the rifle. "It won't cause me one iota of grief to shoot you, mister. Despite what the President thinks, you look more like an abomination than a miracle to me."

They try to force Mr. C into a kneeling position, but he struggles against them until one guy knees him hard in the back. "Lack of respect, wrong attitude, failure to obey authority."

"Please Mr. C," I say, "don't fight them." I turn and look at Grizzly. "They won't hurt me. I'm no good to them dead."

The old guy steps forward and grabs Mr. C's hair, jerking

his head up. "You should listen to little Miss Shannon. She's obviously looking forward to our southern hospitality."

"Fuck you," Mr. C says and spits in the guy's face. The saliva lands on Grizzly's scratched faceplate and dribbles down. The old man stares at it for a minute, then slams the butt of his rifle into Mr. C's head.

"No! Please," I say. "If I cooperate, will you give them fuel and let them go?"

"Why, certainly, young lady," says a new voice.

All the shabby biosuits turn toward a short guy in the only new-looking suit I've seen so far.

"Of course, we will," he says and gives me a slight bow. "I apologize for the over-zealous welcome you've received. Can't be too careful in times like these, and it's been a long time since we've had such enchanting company... Miss Shannon, is it?"

I nod, but get a creepy feeling about him—like he's the smart, handsome guy in a sci-fi flick that turns out to be keeping dead bodies in the freezer of his spaceship.

Mr. New Biosuit nods at the old guy. "Put him in the plane."

"And fill it up with fuel," I say. "Otherwise I won't cooperate."

The guy named Mikey grabs the shoulder of my suit. "Ain't no womenfolk calling the shots around here, missy—less'n of all some low-ranking breeder female."

"Easy there, Brother Michael," the short guy says and puts his hand on Mikey's arm. "She'll learn her place soon enough."

Mikey releases me, and I watch him drag Mr. C back to the plane.

And then I see Madders. He's by a huge truck, his well-cared-for biosuit standing out among the patched and ragtag suits from Catersville. Two guys have him pinned against the truck's door, while another holds a large knife up to the chest of his biosuit.

"Him, too," I say and point at Madders.

"Of course, Shannon, dear. All in God's time." He gestures toward the truck and his men release their captive. Madders starts walking toward us, but Grizzly holds up his rifle. "One more step and you're a dead man."

"It's okay, Madders," I say, trying not to cry. "I'll be fine."

He hesitates. "Shannon, I can't just leave you here."

"Ain't got no choice, flyboy," Grizzly says. "Unless you're fixin to be a martyr."

Madders glances at the plane, then looks back at me, his face tortured. "Shannon—"

"You got one minute before I start practicing my skeet shooting, buddy. Fly or die. Don't make no difference to me."

Huge drops of rain splat against my helmet as Madders starts up the propeller. I watch them stuff Mr. C's limp body into the plane, hoping he's just unconscious and not... worse.

"Tell Mom I love her," I say—even though I know they can't hear me. "And that she was right."

Someone takes my arm and tries to pull me toward the biodome, but I refuse. "I want to see them take off," I say and bite my lip hard—so I don't start crying. "You've stolen my future. The least you can do is let me watch it go."

We stand there in the rain as the plane taxies out to the runway.

"Goodbye, Madders," I say, tears streaming down my face now. "Take good care of Bearhart for me."

"That's enough of that." Someone yanks my arm, pulling me toward the shabby biodome. "We ain't got no tolerance fer crybabies here. Yer a full-grown woman now, and it's time you started acting like one."

A minute later, I can hear more than see the Cessna rise into the dark storm clouds and disappear.

Chapter 25

Diego: Lights Out

When I come to, I hear moaning, and it takes me a minute to realize it's my own. I'm huddled up in a cramped space, the drone of an engine reverberating in my teeth. It hurts to breathe, and my head feels like someone used it as a piñata. I use my sleeve to wipe the caked blood out of my eyes and then look around.

I'm in the backseat of the plane, and it's pitch black, not a single light visible on the ground. I lean forward and look up into Matt's faceplate, the blues and reds of the instrument panel reflecting off it and turning him into some evil alien in a horror movie.

He points to my headset and taps his helmet, and I nod.

With some difficulty, I crawl over into the co-pilot's seat, fasten my seatbelt, and plug in the headphones. "Where's Shannon?"

"They got her," he says. "She managed to convince them to let us go before they marched her inside that wreck of a biodome."

"Christ, Matt. We have to go back!" I'm shaking so badly

the headset slips off and bangs against my knee. "We can't just leave her there with those religious nuts!"

He puts his hand on my leg. "We can't go back, mate. Even if there were something we could do—which there isn't—we don't have enough fuel. Our best bet is to get to C-Bay and convince them to send out a rescue party."

"Fuck."

He pulls Shannon's blanket from the floor behind his seat and hands it to me. "Here. Sorry about the cold. We're up a bit higher than I planned, and it looks like those idiots broke the cowling when they fired off that damn M2, so we're not getting any cabin heat."

I nod, suddenly aware of how cold I am.

"But the engine is fine," he says, "at least so far. I thought about landing to check on the cowling, but I didn't want to waste the fuel."

"How much did they give us?"

"Not enough. We're a bit less than an hour out from C-Bay. Should be able to see the lights soon—assuming we don't run out of fuel first."

"Shouldn't we be looking for a place to land?"

"In ideal conditions, yes. But without a moon, we'd need to be low to the ground to see anything useful, and if we run out of fuel down there, we won't have enough glide to get to safety."

"Christ."

"Best we can do right now is keep our fingers crossed—and hope to hell they know we're out here."

I cover myself with the thin blanket and then stare out into the moonless night, shivering as I watch the stars twinkle in the frigid dark.

I'm sorry, Lani. I know it doesn't mean much now, but I promise I'll get her back. I promise.

Twenty minutes later, the Chesapeake Bay Biodome rises

above the horizon like a full moon, glowing eerily in the pitch-black night.

"That there is one beautiful sight," Matt says. He switches on the radio and makes voice contact a minute later. He gives them our coordinates and adds, "I estimate we're twenty minutes out, tower."

"What's your state, over?"

"Flying on fumes from twenty-year-old unleaded gasoline."

"That shit's gonna fuck up your engine, fife."

"It was that or walk the rest of the way."

"Where'd you let them put that crap in your plane? Over."

Matt briefs them on what's happened. They already know about the Lou, but they had assumed we went back to KC when we didn't land. Turns out, if the plane *had* gone down, they'd never have found us.

"Fife, the manifest says you're transporting Miracle Man and an eighteen-year-old girl. They still with you?"

"Negative. Catersville took Shannon out of the plane at gunpoint," Matt says, his voice sounding hollow. "Diego—that's Miracle Man—fought back, and they beat him up pretty bad. Told us to get out before they opened up with the machine gun. We're lucky most of the fuel was already in the plane when they discovered Shannon, or we'd be gator bait."

"Are you telling me you *left her there*, fife?" There's a waver in the voice of the radio operator. "Son of a bitch, that place is packed full of nut cases. If they tried to take *my daughter*, I'd—"

"Thanks for the advice, tower. We'll let you know when we have visuals on the runway or splash, whichever comes first. Over." He waits for the acknowledgment and then switches off the radio.

"Well," he says. "If we go down now, at least they'll know where to look."

"And then I wouldn't have to tell Lani that we left her

daughter at a backwoods biodome full of religious perverts who plan to force Shannon into sexual slavery."

"Bloody hell, Nadales, it's not as if we had a choice!"

"Yeah, well, you're not the one who convinced Lani to let Shannon come with us."

We fly on in silence, C-Bay slowly filling the horizon.

Until the engine cuts out.

Matt tips the wings, and it roars back to life. "Shite. You may just get your wish, Nadales." He switches on the radio. "C-Bay tower, zero-niner-fife on south-south-west approach, we are out of fuel, over."

"Roger that. We have you on visual, zero-niner-fife. We advise that you glide her in as far as possible. We're scrambling a rescue boat now. Watch out for the gators."

"Alligators? In Virginia?"

"Yes, sir. If you have rocket flares, fire one now and look for the old freeway. There are a few sections still above water, over."

"We copy." He switches to just me. "Damn it, I forgot about those flares from Dulce Base. They're in a plastic box under the seat. Just point the gun barrel out the door, aim as high as you can, and pull the"—the engine cuts out again— "trigger."

I scramble for the box of flares.

"C-Bay approach, zero-niner-fife. We have lost engine power and are going down."

As Matt starts flipping switches and adjusting dials, I set off a flare, lighting up the ground below us. Masses of slithering bodies scramble off an island overpass and back into the dark water.

Mierda.

"There's the raised highway!" Matt says and banks hard to the left.

Two terrifying minutes later, the plane comes to a stop on a short section of dry roadway—no gators in sight.

The flare falls into the water, shrouding us in darkness.

After my eyes adjust, I can see a tiny dot of light moving across the water—way out on the horizon.

Matt nods at me, and I fire another flare.

A minute later, the lights are coming toward us.

Also by DL Orton

Madders of Time Series

Hive

Book One

↓

Jump

(Coming October 2025)

↓

Escape

(Coming April 2026)

↓

Overtime

(Coming October 2026)

↑

Dead Time

↑

Lost Time

↑

Crossing in Time

Between Two Evils Series

About the Author

The Award-winning & Best-selling author
DL Orton lives in the Tropics with her husband, a
golden retriever mix, a Siberian cat, and a bazillion
geckos.

In her spare time, she's building a time machine so that
someone can go back and do the laundry.

Thank You for Reading!
dlorton.com
dlo@dlorton.com

amazon.com/author/dl_orton

bookbub.com/authors/d-l-orton

instagram.com/dl_orton_author

goodreads.com/dl_orton

x.com/dl_orton

facebook.com/DLOrtonWriter

9 781941 368091